About the Author

He is just a simple, hard-working person, now in his retirement years, who has an interest in gardening and general DIY. But since his school days, he always had stories pop up in his mind and now he has decided to write a few down and this is one of them.

Is There Anybody Out There?

Dennis Bagley

Is There Anybody Out There?

Olympia Publishers
London

www.olympiapublishers.com
OLYMPIA PAPERBACK EDITION

A CIP catalogue record for this title is
available from the British Library.

ISBN: 978-1-80439-197-6

This is a work of fiction.
Names, characters, places and incidents originate from the writer's
imagination. Any resemblance to actual persons, living or dead, is
purely coincidental.

First Published in 2023

Olympia Publishers
Tallis House
2 Tallis Street
London
EC4Y 0AB

Printed in Great Britain

Acknowledgements

Thank you to my family for the encouraging way they got me to
get this novel published.

CHAPTER 1

The Bike Ride

Mr Johnson worked in a factory which assembled electronic equipment. On an evening, he would relax by the open fire, telling his two ten-year-old twin boys, Tom and Jack, stories before bedtime. On this particular evening, the rain was hitting the window and a strong wind was howling through the trees. He asked them to turn the TV off and he would tell them a story. Just as Jack was about to switch the TV off, the local news was saying that the police were still no nearer to solving the puzzle of the two missing men from twenty-five years ago.

"That brings back memories. I went to school and worked in the same factory as those two, they were proper clowns until…" He stopped.

"Until what, Dad?" the twins asked, almost in sequence with each other.

Their dad smiled. "Well, I suppose this is tonight's story."

"Is this about the two men that vanished, Dad?" Tom asked very excitedly.

"Yes; that is if you sit still for a while and stop messing about or you're off to bed without a story." They both stopped messing about on the settee.

"It's not me, Dad, it's him." Jack said, hoping to get Tom into trouble.

"Look, just sit still and listen, will you?"

"OK, Dad," they both replied.

Mr Johnson fluffed up the cushions and with a nice cup of tea in his hand he started to tell them the story.

"Many years ago, I was asked to keep a secret by two of my friends, the two missing men. Well, I never took them seriously because they were always messing about, but I think that was mainly because of Jerry; he had a very bad stammer and every word that began with b or w, c, or f... it was sometimes funnier than going to the cinema. Jerry, however, didn't mind people taking the mickey out of him; although Johnny his best friend did sometimes get angry if someone teased him too much.

"What do you mean mickey, Dad?" Jack asked.

"Well, people would mock him and say things like, c-c-can y-y-you, d-d-do. That sort of thing." Dad replied.

"That's not very nice, is it?" Tom said.

"No, but that's how they were then, anyway," said Dad and he continued the story.

"The funny thing is that I have never seen them since: they simply disappeared; err, I think it was sometime in September 1975. They told me about this thing they had found in some old field we used to play in and that it could change the world or something like that. Anyway, it started when we were about your age, perhaps a little older. We were on a bike ride in the summer holidays, in the old village that had the steep hill and a small field, close to a little stream."

Tom jumped up. "Do you mean where Gran used to live Dad?"

"Yes, that's right; the three of us went on a bike ride and everything was fine until we hit the steep hill. Well, for a start our brakes were no good but, for some reason, we just started to pedal down the hill. We went about halfway down and something went wrong. I think a wheel came off someone's bike and we all crashed in a big heap and finished up on the other side of the hedge.

"God, how fast were you going, Dad?" Jack asked.

"Oh, I don't know, pretty fast. Look just be quiet and listen. Well, in this field, very little would grow and animals would not enter anywhere near the far side of the field. It was a strange place and spooky; in fact, it was classed as being evil right back to the middle ages. You know, people even dropped dead in that field."

"Wicked, is it still there, Dad?" Tom asked.

"No, not any longer. It was built on years ago, when the old farmer went missing; come to think about it, he went missing about the same time as Jerry and Johnny."

"Cool, a murder." Jack said, now becoming very interested.

"No, they were never found."

"Taken by aliens from another planet, that's cool."

"I don't think so." Dad replied. "Anyway, listen and I'll tell you about it," he stared at the window, "if I had stayed with them on our bike ride, I might not have been here either."

Mr Johnson went deep into thought and started the story. "Well, it all started back in the summer of 1975," he smiled to himself, "those two lads, were as crazy as crazy can be."

It was halfway through the week in a hot sweaty factory and Jerry Henshaw, who had a bad stammer with B's, D's, P's, and his friend since early school days John Smith, and myself were having our morning tea break, and thinking what to do over the weekend.

"H-h-how's y-your d-d-dad's m-m-motor coming on?"

11

Jerry struggled to say. "He's about as much chance of mending that than the Americans finding rocking horse shit on M-Mars, b-b-but let's be f-f-fair, he did mend your b-b-bike."

"Oh yeah! Can you remember that? When we were going down Baxter Hill on our old bikes and we couldn't stop, because my brakes didn't work and I had to put my shoes onto the front tyre. And pressing as hard as I could to try and stop."

"Ya and they were catching on fire, well at least they were smoking well," Johnny replied.

"You w-weren't m-much b-better, you had y-your f-feet pushing down on the road because you c-c-couldn't stop either." Jerry replied.

"Yeah, and the flipping wheel fell off, the front forks, went into the ground and I shot off like shit off a shovel and landed in that stream covered in cow dung." We all started to laugh.

"Oh yeah! He sorted that out all right. And what about you Johnson, when you ran off because you thought I was dead?" Johnny said, laughing.

"Hey, I f-f-forgot about that and I p-pissed myself with l-l-laughing, can y-you remember?" asked Jerry.

"Yeah and because we took our pants off in that field and hung them on the hedgerow to dry."

"Y-yeah p-piss and s-s-shit, trousers h-h-hanging up to d-d-dry." We all sat laughing about the past.

"You know, I still can't understand what that sound was that made us run off without our pants? And then we had to go back and get our pants so we could go home while you Johnson sat at the top of the hill waiting for us." Johnny said.

"Yeah I'd just h-had a p-piss, and that m-made me want a number two, and no paper." Jerry mumbled while eating his sandwich.

"Ya, and you were pulling your pants up, you pulled up some nettles with them, that made you skip about a bit." Johnny said, laughing.

We had just about finished our Mid-morning break when the manager of the factory came up to us.

"Hey, you pair of silly buggers, get on with your sandwiches and back to work and stop giggling like school girls at play time; come on, get bloody on with it, and you too Johnson, this orders got to be out by tomorrow," said Mr Bagshaw, the manager, in a very agitated voice.

There were only five minutes left of our break we made our way back to the machines.

"Yes, Mister Bagshaw." Johnny turned away and, looking to see if Mr Bagshaw had gone, he turned to Jerry. "Fat bastard, always picking on us two, we'll talk at dinner time."

Just then the blower sounded for the end of tea break and everyone went back to work.

Time soon went by, you were so busy doing work, the time just flew by and soon the lunch blower sounded and everyone found a nice spot in the factory yard and made the best of the warm sunshine.

"What y-yeah got on y-y-your sandwiches, Johnny." Jerry asked while trying to have a peak at Johnny's sandwiches.

"Don't know; tastes like cheese again. What you got?" Johnny replied pulling a face in disgust.

"Cold b-battered f-f-fish," replied Jerry wiping his mouth on the back of his sleeve.

"You dirty bastard, cold fucking fish, you would eat anything.

"It's got salt and v-vinegar on it. Do you want to try some?"

Jerry handed the fish sandwich to Johnny, and with a bit of hesitation, he took a small bite.

"No, take a big bite, so you get the full flavour." Jerry said smiling.

"OK," he put the sandwich in his mouth and took a huge bite.

"Bugger, I didn't mean eat it all you pig."

Munching away on the fish sandwich, Johnny replied, "hey, it's not too bad," he paused and said, "you know it's very strange."

"Well, it should be all right, me mam cooked it last night," he said, looking a bit puzzled.

"Not the fish, what happened to us all that time ago; and it still gives me the shivers." John said.

"M-me to, and h-how m-many years ago was that? Eight or nine?" Jerry replied while trying to think back.

"No, more like fifteen," replied Johnny.

"Shit, was it fifteen, n-never," he replied.

"It was, you know! Hey, Jerry, what about getting the old detectors out and nipping off to that field, see if we can find anything?" Johnny said in excitement.

"I don't know, w-we would need permission, from someone," he said in a very reluctant voice.

"Your bloody scared, you wimp, you daren't go."

"A-arseholes am I! Y-you get p-permission and I'll come with y-you," replied Jerry, hoping Johnny wouldn't get the permission to go.

"Right you're on, I'll phone Sarah at the library in the village and I'll bet she can find out who owns that field, she'll sort it." Johnny said happily, for he didn't mind a trip to the library as Sarah worked there.

"Yeah, she'll s-sort it." There was a worried look on Jerry's face, then silence.

"Y-yes but he does try."

"What the hell are you talking about now?" Johnny asked again, with a confused look.

"Y-your dad, he does try and w-we can't all b-be clever."

"Yeah, I suppose he is a bit clever. Hold on, who else do you know who's clever?"

"Err, n-no one," Jerry replied trying to think of someone.

That evening, Johnny phoned Sarah at home.

"Hello, Mrs Wright, John Smith here, could I speak to Sarah please?"

"Sorry, she's at college until seven thirty. Should I ask her to call you back?"

"Err, no, I'll call round to the college and see her, thanks anyway. Bye!"

Johnny got out his bicycle and made his way to the college. He found Sarah with her friends. As he approached her, he heard one of them saying, "Here's Dumb. Where's Dumber?"

"Hey, there's no need to be like that, they've been good friends to me," she said in an angry voice.

"Can I have a word with you, Sarah?" Johnny asked in a secret whisper while propping his cycle against the hedge.

"Yes, I suppose so," she replied.

"Can you remember the stories about that field on the other side of town?"

"Do you mean the spooky one, where no one goes?" she asked.

"Yes, that's the one. Can you tell me who it belongs to?"

"Johnny, I only work at the library. I don't know every piece of literature that's in there. And I haven't got the time to go through God knows how many bits of information to find that out," she replied.

"No, sorry Sarah. What I meant was, how can I, find out who owns the land?" he replied in a way not to upset her.

"Well if you come in on Friday, I could help you to look through the records and old stories about that field because that's part of my job," she said, smiling.

"That would be great, I'll see you on Friday. Thanks, bye," Johnny said, with a red blushing face. He had a crush on Sarah and while cycling down the road, he almost ran into a car because he was looking back at Sarah.

"You stupid young bugger, look where you're going," the driver shouted and waved his fist at him in anger.

"Sorry." Johnny shouted back, peddling like hell just in case the driver got out to thump him.

The following day, the two lads met up with each other and made their way to the factory.

"Hi J-Johnny. H-how d-d-did you get on with Sarah last n-night then?"

"How the bloody hell do you know about that?"

"I ph-phoned you, b-but yer mam said you had gone out t-to see S-Sarah."

"Well, let's put it this way, after work on Friday we are going to the library and Sarah will get us everything we need and show us all the old newspapers and we can look through them. Sarah said there are loads of stories about that field. And there is also a very old ledger with a lot of information about this area." Johnny told Jerry, but just as they reached the factory gates, two older men started to take the mickey out of Johnny.

"Yo, Johnny baby, get off with Sarah square-eyes then?" asked the first man.

"Bet she's a good mover? Especially with all the sex books she reads every day," said the second.

"Piss off and mind your own business, it was private."

"Y-y-yes m-m-mind y-your own b-b-b-b-business."

"W-well l-listen t-to m-mighty m-mouse," teased the first man.

"Come on Jerry, don't listen to them," said Johnny; giving Jerry a gentle push.

They went into the factory and started to work. Only a few minutes had passed and the loudspeaker was calling them to the office.

"Now what have we done? We're always in trouble for something or the other." Johnny said, brushing his hair.

Putting down their tools they made their way to the manager's office.

"What's wrong, Mr Bagshaw? You wanted to see us?"

"Yes I do, come in. Last week you were on batch number 1232990, the new processor, on those new computers."

"Yes, that's right, but what's wrong?"

"What's wrong? I'll tell you what's wrong. You didn't connect the two main leads on four of these computers. Not only did this blow the machines up but lost £5,000 of data, you are lucky this time they were samples and because the company had back-up facilities. And no harm came from it, you're still here, but the next time anything goes wrong you are both out of here. DO I MAKE MYSELF CLEAR?" Mr Bagshaw shouted.

"Y-yes Mr, Bagshaw, s-sir. Quite c-clear."

"OK, OK get out of here before I lose my temper, and don't let me see you again."

They both left the office feeling ashamed and down in the mouth for what had gone wrong, they were still blaming each other for the poor workmanship, they had done between them.

"Anyway, it's OK him saying it was us, but how the hell are we supposed to understand what these little spiders do, pointing to a poster with a processor on it, everything's getting smaller and smaller. In fact, I think I will soon need specs, I'm getting as blind as a bat these days."

"You sure that's not with seeing Sarah, Johnny boy?"

"On your bike, you shithead." Johnny replied.

"O-only j-joking, o-only j-joking." Jerry said, sniggering to himself.

Well Friday soon came round and the factory closed for halve day. "Listen because when we finish at twelve o'clock, we will go to the library to see Sarah and she will show us the things she has found about that field."

"OK b-but I must ph-phone Mam and t-tell her I will b-be late home." Jerry was no longer smiling.

"OK, but we must get there ASAP because she said there is a load of stuff about that area, and we must read as much as we can, before four o'clock."

They got back to work building the computers but they were teased the rest of the day by the girls in the factory about Sarah the librarian and the mess they had made of the computers, and the bollocking from the gaffer.

"Hey, Johnny, when did you start going out with Sarah posh-specs then?" said a girl on the next bench.

"Does she snog good with her tongue down your throat, or does her specs get in the way?" said another girl that had come to their work bench.

"You d-dirty swine's, that's d-disgusting. P-please g-go or w-we'll b-be in t-trouble again, with fat guts." Jerry replied looking around to see if Bagshaw was looking.

"S-sorry mummy's b-boy, you will have to find out one day that your dick is for more than peeing with," said the first girl.

Just then over the loudspeaker. "Hey, you two girls! Bugger off back to work and stop pissing about with them two. No wonder they get everything wrong!" yelled Mr Bagshaw.

At last, the two lads were left alone and they worked the rest of their shift. The blower sounded for the end of the shift and they quickly made their way to their lockers, grabbed their coats and ran for the bus. As the bus got closer to the village, they decided to get fish and chips for their dinner, as it would be late when they got home.

At the library, they could see Sarah sitting at a large desk with an old gent who was quite well dressed.

"Looks like Sarah's talking to the b-boss, d-do you think she's in t-trouble for getting us those b-b-books?" Johnny looked funny at Jerry.

"The lights on, but no one's in. Jerry, I have to wonder sometimes if you are all there. It's a library, anyone can look at books." Johnny said.

"W-well, I don't know everything," he said in a somewhat simple way.

They walked up to a table, sat at it and it wasn't long before Sarah walked over to them.

"Hello you two, had a hard day?"

Johnny looked up at Sarah's pretty face, and a big soppy grin came across his face. "Yes, it's been quite hard."

"Y-yes, it was quite h-hard to keep our jobs, he's b-been in t-trouble again."

Johnny kicked Jerry under the table. "OK, we have been in trouble, but Sarah isn't interested in that."

"J-J-Johnny, I think y-you like her."

"Shh Jerry, Sarah's," he stopped, as Sarah approached them.

"Sarah's what?" she asked, now with a bright red blushing face, after overhearing Jerry's comments.

Johnny started to blush too. "Jerry, shut up we've—"

"Shh, be quiet," came from people sitting around the library.

Sarah said, "I've put the material you wanted on that table over there, you can photocopy things if you want to. If you need anything, just come across to me and I'll help you out."

Sarah walked back to her desk. All the men reading their books were slyly looking over the tops of their books admiring her hourglass figure.

Jerry looked across at Johnny. "Johnny, we've come for books, not material," he said, looking a little confused.

"Materials as in the books and newspapers, she's found for us, not clothes."

"Oh, I w-wondered w-what she w-was on about. I knew, only k-kidding, J-Johnny. She f-fancies you, Johnny boy, and what a movement." Jerry replied with a cheeky grin on his face.

"Jerry, get reading these papers I want to see if there's anything of interest."

"Yeah, m-me to, God w-what a m-movement." Jerry said, still looking at Sarah's figure.

"Jerry, you'll go blind if you're not careful, ya b-but w-what a risk to take." Johnny said, a little jealous.

There was an awful lot of information about the field. Some of the stories were about ghosts and evil that occupied the field. There was a story about a Roman fort that was destroyed, cows hit by lightning and even people dropping down dead in the field. The list went on and on.

"Blimey, there is certainly something strange going on in that field. I think we should go and have a look around tomorrow. Is your detector working OK?"

"It is, but what about the people that just dropped dead and die just while just walking through the field? Anyway, I need some new batteries; they are going a little flat."

"Come on, Jerry, admit it, you're scared, you don't want to go do you?" Johnny said, taunting him.

"Am not, j-j-just no b-batteries, that's all." Jerry explained.

"Well, that's easy if we run now we can get to the shop before it closes, get some batteries and off we go to the field. So come on, let's go and get some." Johnny said, handing Jerry his coat.

Jerry looked very concerned. Yes, he was scared and so he should be, there was certainly something in that field that shouldn't be there. They walked across to Sarah's desk.

"Should we put away the books, for you Sarah?" Johnny asked, smiling at her as usual.

"No, that's OK, I'll do that for you. Oh and I have found out that the land is owned by a farmer named Mr Wrigley. Can I ask what do you want this information for?"

"We're going looking for lost g-g-gold, J-Johnny seems to think there could be b-buried treasure in that f-field, so we're going with the metal detectors tomorrow." Jerry replied.

"That's a shame, I'm at work tomorrow or I would have come with you. Remember me if you find anything." Sarah said.

"W-we w-will." Jerry said, looking a bit dopey.

"If you don't find anything, perhaps you could take me out for a cup of coffee, or something."

They both stood there with silly smiles on their faces and

said at the same time, "Anytime."

"I'll hold you to that." Sarah said as she gives them a sexy smile, and sly wave making sure no one else sees her.

The two explorers walked out of the library and towards the shops on the other side of the road. Johnny looked back at the library to see if Sarah was still looking at them. But she had gone back to work.

"J-Johnny, is she looking at us? B-boy, if she was coming tomorrow, I would be more than interested," said Jerry as he was about to open the shop door.

"Jerry, you have a one-track mind!"

"I d-do when it c-comes to Sarah."

Jerry turned and looked back to the library and, sure enough, there was Sarah looking up the street at them. Johnny raised his hand and waved to her and she waved back.

"You d-dirty little d-devil, you b-bloody do fancy her. You lying little shit p-p-pot. 'I don't like her and she's too p-posh for me,' you said." Jerry said, teasing Johnny.

"Jerry; for Christ's sake, leave it will you? Course I like her. Who doesn't? Come on, let's get these batteries before this shop closes."

"W-what w-we going in for?"

"Batteries! Detectors tomorrow, you can't have forgotten already? surely not."

"No. I was h-hoping that you had f-forgotten. I'm not t-too sure a-about it," Jerry said, still not happy about going there again.

Inside the newsagents, there were three lads from the college. Johnny tried to ignore them, but they came over in a menacing way.

"H-h-ho l-l-look w-who it is. It's dumb and d-dumber, the

twins again," one lad said.

"Piss off and go and play with each other." Johnny replied.

"Hey, fart face, here's a little advice, keep off the college girls, they belong to us," a second boy said.

"If you m-mean S-S-Sarah, she f-fancies J-Johnny."

"Thanks, Jerry." Johnny said, looking at Jerry while raising his eyebrows.

"Take this as a warning. Keep sniffing around Sarah and you will get into trouble," replied the first college boy.

"The p-police won't d-do anything just b-because we talk to Sarah."

One of the boys got hold of Jerry by the neck then pushed him into a magazine rack. "We are not talking about the police, you clown."

"G-got ya, got ya." Jerry said, pulling himself out of the magazine rack.

The shopkeeper came out from behind the counter. "What the hell are you lot doing? And what's going on here? If you don't get out of my shop, I am calling the police."

"OK pops, don't get in a sweat. We're going," one of the toffs said.

"Can w-we have t-two batteries please?"

"Is that for your sex toy?" a college boy shouted as he went out the shop door.

"I said, get out of here!"

They swung the door wide open and knocked some papers off the counter, shouting abuse to the shopkeeper and finally making their way back to the college.

"Sorry about that." Johnny said.

"It's not your fault. Just because they go to the college, they think they're better than anyone else. Which batteries do you want?" the shopkeeper asked.

"Those please." Jerry said, pointing to two nine-volt batteries.

"That will be £4.99 please, is there anything else you want?"

"Err, two packs of spearmint please."

"So that will be £6.99, please."

"Thank you." Jerry said as he put the money into the shopkeeper's hand.

Putting the batteries in his pocket, they left the shop and made their way home. Johnny arranged to meet Jerry first thing the next morning. He told him not to be late, as they had a lot to cover and he wanted to get the first bus out of town.

CHAPTER 2

The Dig

It was early the next morning. Johnny went around to Jerry's house to make sure he was ready for the big day.

Johnny clinched his fist and knocked very loudly on the front door.

"Jerry! Hey, Jerry, are yea coming?"

Mrs Henshaw popped her head out of the bedroom window. "What the bloody hell do you want at this time in the morning?" she asked in a very angry, tired voice and yawning at the same time.

"Is Jerry coming out to play, Mrs H?"

"You cheeky little bugger! No he is not, it's too bloody early and he is still in bed," she replied.

"But he was supposed to meet me at the bus stop at half six, and he—" Another screeching voice came before he had time to finish.

"Look, are you bloody stupid or what, its bloody Saturday and he is not bloody coming, so bugger off," Mrs Henshaw screeched again.

"Just go and ask him please, he will be very upset if he misses this trip." Johnny shouted back in anticipation.

"What trip?" she asked.

"It's with work; we're off to the seaside for the day, he's booked a seat," trying to think before he knew what he was saying.

"You little bugger, do you think I'm as daft as you? I'll give him a push but if he doesn't wake up, then he isn't coming, OK?" she said in a grumpy voice.

"OK, I'll wait here," he replied.

A few minutes passed and Jerry popped his head round the back door.

"I can't r-remember anything about a t-trip to the s-seaside Johnny," said Jerry, with a big yawn.

"Yes, you can! And don't forget yeah metal detector for the beach," Johnny replied, noticing Jerry's mother peeking behind him.

"OK. B-bloody shit, yeah m-mean we're going to that f-field," he tried to whisper.

"Yes and I have permission from Mr Wrigley the farmer who owns the land. We have got to meet him at between seven thirty and eight, so hurry up: And I think he might be your dad. He's got the same problem as you."

"W-what do you mean?" replied Jerry.

"He s-stutters." Johnny said, laughingly.

"B-but I'm not t-too sure, me m-mam said, it's n-not a nice p-place up there."

"Well it's a good job your mam's not coming, isn't it. Just get yeah nick-nick and let's bugger off, before we miss the bus. Mr Wrigley is waiting for us," Johnny said, getting very grumpy.

Reluctant to go, Jerry stood for a few minutes, went back inside, got dressed and came back out with his metal detector.

"Oh, bugger it, we're not kids any more and I do want to see what's in that field. If anything at all that is." Johnny said, while making their way to the bus stop.

"Come on, Jerry, let's go. Hey, do you know what Neil Armstrong said when he landed on the Moon?"

"I don't know, I didn't see the f-film. I give up." Jerry said, not yet awake.

"No, he didn't say that. He said there's no way a bloody cow jumped over here."

"He didn't. Did he?" Jerry replied, not even knowing about the Moon landing.

"Bloody hell, Jerry; hey diddle, diddle, the cat and the fiddle, the cow jumped over the Moon."

"Hey!" he replied, scrunching up his face.

"Oh, forget it. Come on, let's go," said Johnny, shaking his head. The two friends ran down the road kicking an empty can, and talking about what they would do if they found anything valuable.

Jerry glanced up. "Johnny! The b-bus is here!"

"Come on, you prat, we'll miss it," Johnny said, kicking the tin can down the road.

They ran like hell, holding their hand out, hoping the diver would see them and stop the bus.

"You nearly missed it," the bus driver said, smiling.

"It's this plonker. He can't get out of bed."

"You'll have to leave it alone, sonny, if you can't get up this early," the bus driver said, chuckling.

"Leave what alone?" Jerry said with a confused look on his face.

"Forget it, Jerry. Two to Wrigley's Farm please." Johnny asked, holding out the money.

"£1.50 please," the driver replied.

"Christ, that's nearly an hour's wage." Johnny said, a bit disgusted.

"I know, but look at the entertainment you get with it," the driver replied.

They made their way to the back of the bus, holding on to the seats.

Johnny rang the bell and shouts to the driver. "Carry on, my good man, and don't spare the horses!"

"Press that bloody bell once more and I'll kick you off," the driver said, angrily.

"Sorry," he said in an apologetic voice.

"Yes, well, it's more than my job's worth," replied the driver.

The driver turned to face the front and slowly started to crunch the gears into place, with a loud crunching sound, the bus jolted forwards and started to move. They were forced to the back of the bus and landed on the back seat. They turned to look out of the back window and started pulling faces at a policeman peddling his bicycle up the steep hill. The red-faced policeman was so mad he lost control of his bike and almost fell off. It took about thirty minutes to arrive at Wrigley's Farm.

Getting off the bus, that had stopped right outside the farm; they could see Farmer Wrigley in the farmyard sat on a bench, under an apple tree, eating a sandwich. They opened the gates and walked in.

"Hello." Johnny said to the farmer.

"W-who are y-you?" replied Mr Wrigley.

"Oh no, I don't think I can put up with two of you." Johnny said, under his breath, and thinking how hard is this conversation going to be.

"W-what are y-you on about?" the farmer replied.

"H-he m-means M-m-me."

"W-why you ch-cheeky little b-bugger. Go on, g-get out of

here, I'm s-sick of p-people taking the p-p-piss out of me. Go on, b-before I set the dogs on ya," Mr Wrigley said in a very nasty voice.

"Mr Wrigley, he stutters as well, he's not taking the piss," Johnny quickly replied, hoping not to upset Mr Wrigley.

"Oh well that's different, you g-get a lot of p-people taking the p-piss you know," he replied.

"Y-yes, Mr Wwwigly, I know h-how you feel. The girls at work are the worst."

"Anyway, w-what can I d-do f-for you two?" he asked.

"Well, Mr Wrigley, I phoned you yesterday teatime and you said it would be OK for us to go into that field down by the rocks. We would like to try out our metal detectors to see if we can find anything," Johnny said, while sitting down on the bench by the side of Mr Wrigley.

"With yer whats?" Mr Wrigley asked.

"Metal detectors. They find metal things in the ground." Johnny replied.

"W-what d-do they d-do, suck t-things out of the ground?" Mr Wrigley said with a confused look.

"No, it would be nice but we have to dig things out with our trowels." Johnny replied taking a small trowel out of his rucksack.

"W-what w-will it f-find then?" replied Mr Wrigley.

"Old swords, coins, copper pipes, anything made of metal."

"It's m-mainly tin c-cans, b-bottle tops, n-nails, etc."

"Hey, lads, I don't know, what will they come up with next? N-Now then, let's say y-you f-find gold or a d-diamond brooch, or other t-treasure, who g-gets it?" asked Mr Wrigley.

"We share it, Mr Wrigley! Three-way split, a third each." How do's that sound?" Johnny replied.

"Y-yes, a three-w-way split." Jerry repeated.

"W-well, that s-sounds fair. OK, it's a d-deal, b-but that field has n-never had anybody on it f-for years, not even a c-cow will go in that p-part of the f-field. I hear some s-say it's haunted. Do you s-still want to go in there?"

"Yes please, we'll be all right, and we promise to fill any holes we make." Johnny told him.

"W-well, I'll see y-you later w-when you b-bring me my share of the treasure." Mr Wrigley laughed so hard his face turned bright red.

The two lads walked away from Mr Wrigley saying, "See you later, and a nice pot of tea wouldn't go a miss," Johnny said, laughingly.

They made their way through the other small farmyard gate that lead down to the strange field.

"If we start at the far end of the field and then make our way back up to the farm that will be best." They made their way over the stiles and walked down the footpath towards the field.

"Jerry, this looks like the place where we came through the hedge, don't you think. Yep, this is it all right. I've got a feeling in my water." Johnny said.

"You've n-not p-pissed yourself again h-have you?" Jerry replied.

"Very funny. That looks like the hill we came down and the hedgerow where we came through into the field." Johnny said, pointing to the steep hill on the other side of the hedge.

"Yeah y-you're right, t-this is the right p-place." Jerry said, taking his detector out of his carrier bag.

They searched the area for about two hours. They covered lots of places all around the field and were beginning to get fed up. They had found nothing. Not even a can, not even a blip sound.

"Sh-should w-we go, Johnny?"

"Not yet, another hour and we'll call it a day." Johnny said in a disappointed voice.

"Hey, y-you two! Got s-some tea, and b-biscuits, that's if you're interested!" Mr Wrigley shouted from over the stone wall.

"Wicked, thanks, Mr Wrigley. That's very kind of you," Johnny replied. The two lads sat on the stonewall drinking their tea and having a chat with Mr Wrigley. "How long have you owned this land Mr Wrigley?"

"It's b-been in my family f-forever, it goes b-back hundreds of y-years." Mr Wrigley replied.

"W-we've heard some s-stories about this f-field, and some are v-very s-spooky." Jerry said.

"S-spooky; I can t-tell you s-some stories all right, they'll freeze ya b-bones," replied Mr Wrigley.

"Go on then, Mr Wrigley, tell us some." Johnny said, eagerly.

Taking a sip of tea and bite of his biscuit, he said, "Well, you see d-down there w-where that bump is," he pointed down the field, "m-many years ago, m-my great g-granddad, was trying to p-plough this field with two v-very big shire horses. The p-plough blades got s-stuck on something and the plough started to glow red and then v-vanished."

"Vanished?" Johnny asked.

"V-vanished into thin air, the plough just m-melted away, the two horses ran w-wild, reared up and kicked poor granddad to d-death. After t-that, everyone who w-walked through this field s-said that they could see coloured l-lights shining out of the ground and could hear s-strange noises. The s-same thing happened a-again in World W-War Two, a G-German plane d-dropped a b-bomb on the f-field, made a large h-hole and again, bright lights were seen in the field. Can't s-say that I've ever seen a-anything but that's the s-story." Mr Wrigley told them.

"What about the stories in the library, they go back hundreds of years. There are stories about people seeing ghosts, strange lights and sounds, all coming from this field." Johnny replied, thinking back to the stories in the library.

"That's w-what I told you, it's h-haunted." Mr Wrigley laughed.

"Can I tell you something, Mr Wrigley?" Johnny asked.

"Yes." Mr Wrigley replied.

"When we were kids, we were on a bike ride and we came down that steep hill. We had an accident, came off the bikes, came through the hedge and landed in your field. We heard very weird noises in this field and that's why we are interested, but when you tell anyone they just laugh at you." Johnny told him.

"B-bloody hell, Johnny. L-let's call it a d-day. I'm getting spooked." Jerry said, becoming very nervous.

"No, we'll have a few more hours and see what happens, if we don't find anything, we'll go home," he replied, jumping over the wall for a pee.

Jerry asked, "Is there any more sandwiches left?"

Johnny reached down into his rucksack. "One," he shouted.

"Can I have it?" Jerry replied, still sitting on the wall.

"Yeah, here catch." Johnny shouted back. He tossed the bag to Jerry, it went a little high Jerry reached up to catch it, but he went back too far and fell backwards over the wall.

"Huff," came a sound from Jerry as he fell backwards over the wall.

"Are you all right, Jerry?" there was no answer. "Are you

all right, Jerry?" Still no answer. "Jerry? Are you all right?" There was still no answer.

Jerry had fallen down a grass bank and started to make his way back to the top. As he reached the wall, he looked over the top, just as Johnny was about to shout again.

"Jerry, are you all ri—?" he suddenly stopped.

Jerry jumped up. "BOO!" Johnny fell backwards and rolled onto the grass.

"You stupid bastard, I could have died, you could have given me a heart attack!" Johnny said, but found the funny side of it.

They couldn't do anything for laughing. Even Mr Wrigley found it funny. His face was as red as a cherry with laughing.

"Ee, by gum, lad. I haven't s-seen anything so f-funny for ages that was v-very funny." Mr Wrigley said.

They all started laughing.

"Well, you two, I must get on. I'll see you later," he said, turning to make his way back to the farm.

"Bye, see you before we go!" Johnny shouted.

Mr Wrigley walked away still laughing. "OK, y-you're a pair of silly b-buggers."

"Come on, Jerry, let's have another go."

"OK," came a nervous reply.

They walked down the field to the bump in the ground that Mr Wrigley told them about and started their search again. This time, they start under the stone wall on the grass banking, walking towards the hump and came away from the wall. Johnny got a very strong signal.

"Jerry, come over here I've found something!" Johnny shouted beckoning him over.

"W-what is it? S-shit, it's that W-world War Two b-bomb!"

"Don't be a prat, it's huge, look," he said as he waved the detector backwards and forwards over a large area and walked around the large circular area.

"Jerry, you walk over that way and see where it stops beeping."

Jerry started to walk away from Johnny working the metal detector from side to side.

"It's v-very b-big, Johnny."

"Let's get some twigs from out of the hedge and we can walk from side to side, and when the signal stops, we can push a stick into the ground and mark it out."

"That's c-clever."

After about an hour or so, they placed the last twigs.

"Let's go up the bank and see what it looks like."

"Yeah." Jerry replied now becoming more excited.

They climbed to the top of the bank and climbed up onto the stonewall. Looking down, they could see a perfect huge circle.

"Shit!" they both said at the same time.

"That's some coin, Jerry." Johnny said, looking up at Jerry who had his mouth wide open.

"Let's dig." Johnny said, jumping off the wall and running down to the circle.

They took their small trowels out of their rucksacks and started to dig. Digging down was a little harder than they thought it would be with just a couple of small trowels. What they needed was a shovel. Johnny went to the farm for a shovel. Jerry sat there looking at this huge circle. He said to himself, "What the hell is this? I'm getting butterflies again."

Johnny returned with a spade and shovel. "What did you say, Jerry?"

"I said, I'm getting butterflies again."

"Don't be a prat Jerry, pull yourself together."

Picking up the tools, they started to dig. It hadn't been long before they thought they heard the strange sounds again. "Is that the same sounds we heard when we were in the field all those years ago, Johnny?"

"Jerry, something's got me." Johnny said as he bent down into the soil.

"Pack it in, you're scarring me, you prat."

"Did you ask if you could borrow these spades?" asked Jerry.

"No, Mr Wrigley was out so I borrowed them, we'll take them back later. What's up, Jerry? You look like you've seen a ghost." Johnny asked as he looked across at Jerry.

"Johnny, shush. Listen."

Johnny stood across from Jerry, straining his ears to listen, but didn't hear anything.

"Listen, listen to that, I d-don't like t-this, s-something's not r-right."

"Yes and I'm looking at him. Come on, let's dig a bit more out, there has got to be something in here."

"Come here, Johnny, come and s-sit here. C-come on s-sit here."

Johnny moved across to where Jerry was sitting and sat by the side of Jerry.

"Jerry, what the hell is that? It sounds like voices, or a choir singing, this is weird." Johnny said, looking around to see if he could see anyone, or anything.

"Should we go?"

"No, no, not yet. Let's dig a little first." Johnny started to dig down. He went down about two to three feet.

"Come on, Johnny, let's p-pack in for t-today."

"Not till I've found something metal. Anyway, it's your turn, come on get down here." Johnny said, passing the spade to Jerry.

They swapped places and Jerry started to dig down. After a few shovels, clonk!

"I've found something, come down."

He jumped down into the hole.

"What have we found?" Johnny asked with excitement.

"D-don't know, b-but it sure is m-metal."

"Look at it, it's shining, and it looks like new," Johnny said, brushing away the soil.

"Is it something to d-do with the army? A b-bunker or s-s-something l-like that, do you think?" Jerry asked in a worried voice.

"No, don't think so, let's move some more soil."

They cleared a larger area from around the metal. Johnny removed one of his gloves.

"I can't understand why it looks so new, it's obvious it's been here for years. Look at these markings, it's Egyptian or something."

He brushed away some more soil from the metal. As he did, there was a blue glow between his hand and the metal. Johnny started to shake.

"Come on, Johnny, let's go."

"Not yet, Jerry. Look at this," he moved his hand closer and the blue glow now made an aurora around his hand. He turned to Jerry. "Look at this," he said as he started to move his hand even closer.

"Come on, Johnny, I'm g-getting a horrible f-feeling about b-being here."

"OK," he replied with a chuckle in his voice, we will have to come tomorrow. Give me a pull-up.

"Come on, stop m-messing about."

"I can't. It's pulling me."

"Johnny, let go." Jerry shouted as he tried his hardest to pull him away from the blue glow.

"I can't pull harder!" Johnny was now very worried.

Jerry took hold of Johnny's hand, only to find that he was also being pulled towards the metal. Suddenly, they were both thrown through the air and out of the hole.

"Shit, I t-told you I didn't l-like this, I feel so weak," Jerry said, sweat running down his face.

"Me too, let's pack up and go, I'm wet through, I don't like this one little bit."

"Get Mr Wrigley's shovels and let's get out of here." Johnny said.

Johnny looked down into the hole to see Mr Wrigley's shovels, leaning against the shiny metallic object. "I'm sure we just dropped them," he jumped down into the hole. As he did, the ground started to rumble and the metal started to slowly rotate in the hole.

"W-what the b-bloody hell is h-happening now?" asked Jerry, as the object stopped revolving.

"It's stopped, Jerry. There are some lights on it."

"W-what do you m-mean?"

"Lights. Four lights in a row!"

"Where did they come from?"

"Search me." Johnny said moving forwards to touch the lights. There was a slight vibration through the ground. He pulled back.

"Johnny, leave it alone, let's go, throw the spades out to

37

me."

"Hold on, Jerry. I'm just going to touch a light, that's all." Johnny slowly moved down into the hole and placed his finger near the top light. A slight vibration could be felt through the ground again.

"Something's happening." Jerry said.

Touching another button, another vibration could be felt through the ground, but nothing else happened.

"Perhaps you should press them at the same time and see if you get another shock?"

"Perhaps, you should press them at the same time." Johnny said.

"OK." Jerry told him to move out the way as he jumped down into the hole.

"God, you're a brave sod all of a sudden, come out the way." Jerry pressed all four buttons at the same time, there was that sound again like a choir singing a chord and the ground started to vibrate once more.

"That was nice! Play me something else, but there is still nothing happening."

"I b-bet it has to b-be in a sequence l-like a chord on a k-keyboard." Jerry said, seeming quite the professional.

"Christ, listen to Jerry Mozart, the great composer!"

"Look, let's try a few and see what happens."

"OK, but we can't stay much longer it's going to get dark soon and the last bus will be here. If we miss that one we will have to catch the town bus and walk two miles back home."

"OK, b-but we m-must keep t-trying. This m-must do something it m-might even be a way in."

They both tried pressing the buttons in different sequences but nothing happened. They were about to give up when Jerry pressed the buttons in sequence then pressed all the buttons at the same time while leaning with one hand on the silver metal. Something started to happen.

"Johnny, come here and feel the metal, its giving a tingling feeling." Jerry said, giggling.

Johnny stood at the side of Jerry and placed both hands on the metal surface. The ground now shook more violently.

"Jerry, I think it's time to go." Johnny said, now very nervous.

Then suddenly, like magic, the metal seemed to dissolve leaving a threshold into the object.

"Shit, it's a doorway. It looks like a secret room in there." Johnny said, excitedly.

"Shit is the word, let's get going." Jerry had now changed his mind and didn't want to stay any longer.

"L-let's look inside, you m-mean?" Jerry said, now being the braver of the two.

Slowly poking his head inside the dim opening, the inside started to get brighter; he pulled his head out and looked over the hump.

"That's impossible, Jerry."

"W-what is?" he replied.

"You just put you head in there." Johnny said.

"W-what for? It's d-dark. You can't h-hardly see a-anything."

"Just put your head inside will you, it's quite safe." Johnny said, reassuringly.

Jerry put his head inside; again the inside of the object lit up and there in front of him was a long passageway.

"This doesn't m-make sense."

"I told you so."

"Look how far across it is out here. Yet inside, it's huge."

Jerry looked over the top of the hump.

"It's huge inside b-but small o-outside, how can that b-be?"

"Don't know, but I'm going in to have a good look around. You coming or stopping out here?"

"OK, b-but if anybody c-comes, it was y-your idea."

They got back down in the hole and looked inside again.

"Are you sure about this?" Jerry asked, walking very sheepish into the opening. They could see that the passage way went quite a long way into darkness.

"D-do you think w-we should get M-mr Wrigley. After all, it is his field, it m-might be something of his, and w-we don't want to g-get in any trouble." Jerry explained.

"Oh, now who's scared?"

"No, I'm not. I j-just don't w-want to get into any trouble."

"Mr Wrigley doesn't know about this, that's for sure."

"M-maybe you're right, b-but there's no light a-any further down than w-what we can see." Jerry said, trying to get out of venturing any further.

"I suppose you're right, but what about the opening? We can't leave it like this. Someone else might find it and we don't know what it is do we?" Johnny said, now being convinced by Jerry, to leave and go home.

As they turned away and started to climb out the hole to leave, they could hear someone speaking, it was a strange sounding voice, not in English.

"Did you here that Jerry?" Johnny said, startled.

"Yeah, it c-came from in t-there," he replied.

"Let's go, Jerry." Johnny said and was starting to panic.

"M-maybe you're right. W-we could come b-back tomorrow. We c-could leave the detectors with Mr Wrigley and g-get a taxi." Jerry said, now in full agreement with Johnny.

Something started to happen. Their feet felt like they were stuck in mud. They tried to pull themselves free but fell to their knees. They were now very worried. As they started to fall towards the metal object, they put their hands out so as to not hit their faces on the metal. Their outreached hands touched the metal object and again they could feel that something was draining their energy, and it felt like a magnet had stuck them to it. They were feeling very tired.

"Johnny, t-this is no l-longer fun; I'm beginning t-to feel very w-weak." Jerry told Johnny.

Their hands were no longer stuck to the metal and they fell back.

"Me too, Jerry. Let's just sit for a while and get our strength back, and we could probably make our away out."

They rested a while waiting, hoping to recover some of their strength.

"It seems like we have been here for ages, should we try and move?"

Suddenly a bright beam of intense light scanned across their faces. This made them both jump, but they found that they could now move quite easily.

"W-what the h-hell was t-that, Johnny? W-was it lightning?"

"Beats me, but I'm not very happy about being here. What is this place?"

"Maybe if we had some light it would be a little better—" But before Jerry had finished speaking, the whole passageway was lit, yet there was no direct light. It seemed to be coming from out of the walls.

"How the hell did you do that, Jerry?"

"I d-don't know. Hey, d-don't you b-blame me for t-that. It was as th-though it knew what I was th-thinking."

"Look down there, Jerry, it seems to go for ever." Come on we have come this far, let's have a little look, and then we'll turn back."

"I've never seen anything like it, it's so weird."

They got to their feet and made their way down the passage. On the walls down the full length of the passageway were symbols like hieroglyphics. Again, part of the wall dissolved to reveal another opening into another room. It was full of panels, covered in an array of coloured lights. There were monitors on the walls. And it was certainly something that they had never seen before.

In front of them were three high-backed chairs. Jerry took hold of the top of the centre one and spun it round at the same time he said, "Scotty, to bridge." As the chair swivelled around, the skeleton remains of a creature fell from the chair and knocked him to the floor.

"Ahh, Johnny I've been got. Run! No, help me! Oh, shit, what we going to do?"

"Now you've gone and done it." Johnny said scared stiff and not daring to move.

"Johnny, p-please g-get it off." Jerry shouted, now in a state of panic.

Johnny looked down at the skeletonised body, which was pinning Jerry to the floor.

"Jerry, it's not one of us."

"N-no it's d-dead and I d-didn't kill it, help me up," he replied.

"No, you dickhead. It's not human."

"Oh s-shit, Johnny. Get it off, please, it weighs a tonne."

42

Jerry started to move the bones off him and Johnny started to help.

"What have we found?"

"D-don't know, b-but somehow I feel like we s-should be here."

"Me too. I've got a feeling of well-being and content."

The sense of well-being became stronger and they were no longer afraid to be there, to the extent of a warm glow inside. They looked down at the strange shape on the floor. It had two legs and two arms; the arms were somewhat longer than theirs, the skull had a pointed chin and large eye sockets and the forehead were bulging as if it encased a much larger brain.

"You k-know what, Johnny, this is so cool." Jerry said in a calm voice.

A voice started to say things in many different kinds of languages, and finished in English.

"This is so cool," a slurred voice repeated.

They looked startled at each other.

"T-that's not m-me."

"That's not me," the voice repeated again.

"What the hell is going on, Jerry?"

"What the hell is going on, Jerry?" the voice said in broken English.

"Who are you? Come on, show yourself." Johnny shouted with a little fear in his voice as he looked around the room to see if anyone else was there.

There was no answer; there was a deadly silence, then suddenly, "This is voice recognition, Earth, more advanced, what year?"

"Jerry, it's talking to us."

"This is voice recognition, Earth, more advanced, year?"

the voice asked in broken English.

The pair just stood there, looking at each other.

"Year, year, year, year?" the voice repeated over and over.

"For Christ sake, 1975." Johnny replied, a little grumpy.

"Christ; Jesus; Son; Lost; cannot find, searching data." Then silence. A few seconds passed. "One thousand nine hundred and forty-six years have passed. Processing information," the voice said. "No records found, insufficient power, need more power. Please sit."

"No, thank you, we need to go." Johnny said in a somewhat rushed voice.

"Y-yes we n-need to go," said Jerry.

"Yes need to go, please sit," the voice responded still in broken English.

"There's n-no seats." Jerry said, and thought he wasn't sitting in that skeletons seat. But, before he could finish the sentence, the other two seats turned to face them.

"Shit." Johnny said, getting a bit more worried.

"Human body function; disposal incineration unit none functional, power low," the voice replied.

Jerry laughed. "Hey, he's quick. It's got a sense of humour too."

"Please, sit," repeated the voice in a gentler mood.

"Err, no, we have to go, or we will." Johnny couldn't speak it was like something had stopped him speaking and they couldn't move their limbs.

They were pulled towards the two seats by some sort of power they had no control over and they were made to sit down. Again, a bright light scanned their faces and they couldn't move. The beam went horizontal then vertical several times. Out of the wall came two very thin mechanical arms, with something like suction cups on the ends and a small fluorescent glowing ball in the end of each cup. Slowly, the arms moved towards their faces. They tried to move but it was impossible, it was like being stuck in a pot of sticky glue. The probes started to work their way up their nostrils, their eyes started to water as the probe moved from side to side and moved further inside their nose. Then, with a sudden thrust, it was manoeuvred into place. An intense beam of light shone into their eyes and onto their foreheads, there was a great pain in their heads. They both shook violently until they lost consciousness. After what seemed to be a few minutes they both came round.

"Thank you, you will now start to understand many things but don't worry, I will be here to help you. You will return and you will bring them with you on your return, we can then start our search again," the voice said.

"Bring what with us?" Johnny asked.

"You will understand." The lights started to dim and the screens began to fade, and with a whining noise the life of the craft began to fade. It was as though the machine was going to sleep.

"C-come on, Johnny, l-let's get out of here."

They stood but were very shaky and made their way to the entrance. They almost dropped out of the door and into the hole outside and fell to the ground. Once outside, they got their breath back and adjusted their eyes to the outside. They soon noticed, however, it was dark. All they could see was a faint light coming from the farmhouse. They had no idea how long they had been inside the craft but it didn't seem to have been that long.

"Phew! D-did that r-really happen, Johnny?" Jerry said as he turned around to have a look at the metal object.

"It's gone!"

"What has gone?"

"The opening. It's n-not there." Jerry replied in a shocked voice.

Johnny turned to have a look. "How has that happened?"

"I d-don't know but m-my head's sore." Jerry said, rubbing his forehead.

"Come on, we better make our way to Mr Wrigley's before it gets too dark. I have a headache too," replied Johnny.

They picked up the spades and metal detectors and staggered up to the farmhouse. In the distance, they could see the light was on in the kitchen. When they arrived back at the farm, they placed the spades against the wall where Johnny had found them and went to the kitchen door. Jerry took hold of the doorknocker and hit the door a few times.

"Who is it?" shouted Mr Wrigley.

"It's us, M-mr Wrigley," shouted Jerry.

The kitchen door slowly opened and Mr Wrigley peered out of the door. "Well, b-blow me, I thought you t-two had gone home ages ago," Mr Wrigley said, wiping his mouth on his sleeve.

"No, we hit a spot of trouble," replied Johnny.

"T-trouble, yeah? B-best come in. D-do you want a cuppa?" said Mr Wrigley, opening the door wider.

He opened the door and led them in. He was surprised how pale they both were and they had two red marks on their foreheads. "Trouble? L-looks l-like you've had a r-round with a boxer, y-you've b-both got nose bleeds, and t-two lovely red b-bumps on your heads, hhere, I'll m-make a cheese sandwich," Mr Wrigley said, while getting the cheese out the fridge.

Johnny raised his hand to his heads. He could feel two little bumps there, and it was very sore.

"Ouch, that stings." Johnny said, touching the bumps.

"They do look sore, Johnny. Mine feels a little tender too," Jerry said, reaching up to his head.

"I d-don't know about that, b-but what I do kn-now you have m-missed the last b-bus," said Mr Wrigley.

"We'll get the next bus, to town and walk the rest of the way." Johnny replied.

"No, you've missed the last bus, its five to twelve, the last bus is eleven thirty."

"Bugger, now what?" Johnny replied.

"Y-you can s-stop here f-for the night, it will have to b-be on the sofa though, and y. You can ring your m-mum's first and I can t-take you home f-first thing in the morning, h. Here, h-have a c-cheese sandwich," said Mr Wrigley passing them a plate full of sandwiches.

"Thank you, Mr Wrigley, for your hospitality." Johnny said, munching on a sandwich. They phoned home and started to tell Mr Wrigley about what had happened, but they slowly drifted off to sleep. Mr Wrigley placed a blanket over them, took the plate out of Johnny's hand and smiled as he looked at them both fast asleep on the sofa. He switched off the light and went to bed.

The next morning, Mr Wrigley walked into the room. "Well, h-have you had a good n-night's rest?" Asked Mr Wrigley.

"Yes, not too bad, but my head still hurts." Johnny said, rubbing his head.

"So does m-mine." Jerry commented getting up from the sofa.

"Yes, and b-by the look of t-them bruises, you must h-have

47

got a fear old w-whack," said Mr Wrigley in a jolly voice.

"Whack? We didn't bump our heads, did we?" He stopped talking for a minute, he didn't know what to say.

"Err, don't know what we did, but it hurts like hell still," Johnny butted in quickly.

"P-Perhaps you should—" Mr Wrigley said, making a cup of tea, but was interrupted.

"No, we don't need a doctor thanks, Mr Wrigley." Johnny said abruptly.

"H-How did you kn-now I was going to say that?" Mr Wrigley asked, looking confused.

"I don't know, I just knew what you was going to say," replied Johnny.

"L-Look, lads, go to the d-doctors and see w-what they say. Those t-two bumps look a bit n-nasty." Mr Wrigley replied, looking at their heads.

"OK, if it's still there tomorrow we will go and see what's wrong." Johnny replied.

"That's b-better, now go and get a w-wash the bathrooms, s-second door on your left, and I'll get some b-breakfast for us and y-you can tell me about w-what treasures you found," said Mr Wrigley, putting some bacon and eggs into the frying pan.

They got up and went upstairs to wash. In the bathroom, they looked into the mirror to see the bumps on their heads that Mr Wrigley was talking about.

"Hells bells, how do we explain this to everyone?" Johnny asked Jerry.

"D-don't know, b-but me m-mam will want to kn-now, you kn-now what she's like." Jerry said, looking up to the ceiling and shrugged his shoulders.

"I don't know what we will tell Mr Wrigley? Jerry, do we

tell him the truth?"

"The truth? Now you're the loony tune, he will think were bonkers." Jerry replied.

Just then, Mr Wrigley shouted upstairs to say that their breakfast was on the table and that they should phone their mothers to let them know that they were going to be home a bit later. They made their way down to the breakfast table where Mr Wrigley was sitting with a cup of tea and a bacon sandwich.

"H-Help yourselves. T-there's b-bacon, sausages and e-eggs, I m-make my own b-bread so you will h-have to cut it." Mr Wrigley said, munching on a rather thick bacon sandwich.

"Thanks, Mr Wrigley, it looks wonderful."

"Yes, thanks."

They both sat down to eat and eat they did until everything was wiped clean. Even the juice on the plate was dabbed up with a nice slice of homemade bread.

"Mr Wrigley, that was wonderful. It's the best meal I've ever had!"

"Yes, m-me too." Jerry said with a loud burp.

"D-Don't call me, Mr Wrigley. Call me Jack."

"OK, Mr, err, J-Jack." Jerry said with a snigger. "Is it OK to phone my mam, Jack?" Jerry smiled, that sounds strange, he thought.

"Yes, sure you can. And Johnny can tell me what was keeping you so busy all day." Mr Wrigley said as he was pouring up three cups of tea.

They both looked at each other as much as to say now, "what do we tell him?"

"Well then, what did you find?" Mr Wrigley asked.

"Err, it's not that simple." Johnny said, trying to think of how to tell him in a simple way.

"C-come on lad, we're f-friends, and we d-did say we w-would share everything." Jack smiled.

"Well, you will not believe us if we tell you." Johnny replied.

"T-Try me." Jack said.

"Do you live here by yourself, Jack?" Jerry asked as he burst into the room from talking to his mam on the phone. Johnny quickly jumped up and went to phone his mam.

"Y-Yesterday, tell me about y-yesterday and I'll t-tell you about me." Jack replied, getting a little anxious.

Jerry was just about to start when Johnny came back into the room. "Mam said it was OK, as long as she knows I'm OK and as long as I'm home for tea."

Knowing they had to tell Jack something, Johnny gave a little smile.

"That's OK, then you c-can tell me all about w-what you f-found. Come on t-then sit down and t-tell me w-what you got up to." Jack asked eagerly.

"OK, Mr Wrigley."

"It's Jack."

"Sorry, I forgot. It doesn't seem right."

"OK, if t-that's what you w-want." Mr Wrigley replied.

"Y-yes, I feel m-more comfortable with M-Mr Wrigley somehow." Jerry replied.

"Yes me too." Johnny said, trying to get out of telling him what had happened.

"W-Well, c-Come on then." Mr Wrigley said.

"OK, but you won't believe us." Jerry replied.

Jack looked over his specks and took a deep sigh.

"OK, here goes."

The two boys told Mr Wrigley everything. He sat there in

somewhat of a daze, got up and looked down the field through the kitchen window.

"So, t-this is in my f-field is it?"

"Yes. W-We said you w-wouldn't believe us." Jerry explained.

"Oh, b-but I do lads."

"You do?" Johnny said, surprised.

"Yes, I have kn-nown for some time t-that there was s-something out there like that."

"Why haven't you ever looked for it?"

"I have. M-Many years ago. It almost sent m-me mad and I even l-lost my wife and d-daughter through it."

"D-did they l-leave you, Mr Wrigley?" Jerry asked, in sad voice.

"N-No, they were both killed in the fire," replied Mr Wrigley.

"Oh, so sorry, Mr Wrigley. What happened?"

"Jerry, Mr Wrigley doesn't want to talk about that, and it's none of our business."

Mr Wrigley bent down and put on the radio, it was a classical programme. The presenter said he was going to play Mendelssohn's violin concerto.

"We'll l-listen to that. It's m-my favourite p-piece of music." Mr Wrigley said.

"If you don't want to tell us, we understand."

"Yes, if it's too hard for you, then don't bother, Mr Wrigley."

"No, it was m-many years ago. It still hurts b-but I can tell you. It s-sometimes helps to talk a-about it." Mr Wrigley said and started to tell them about what happened.

"W-Well, it was a-about forty years ago, around about

1956. Like you, I h-heard the strange noises m-many times, but I could never find a-anything. I s-spent days d-digging and looking, d-digging and looking, and after m-many months I found something in the s-same spot where you w-were looking. I was so b-busy trying to clear the ground away, I n-never noticed the h-house was on fire. As I looked up, I could see m-my Jenny and little Amy s-standing at the b-bedroom window s-screaming for me t-to help. B-but the flames l-licked around t-them. I ran to the house b-but there was n-nothing I could do. Oh G- god, I'm sorry Jenny, so sorry." Mr wrigley said, sobbing and wiping away the tears.

Both Jerry and Johnny were also wiping their tears away they both looked at him, not knowing what to say or do.

Mr Wrigley continued, "I stood t-there without a t-thought in my mind, it was empty. N-Nothing left and nothing worth l-living for. I have n-never been so sad and so, so empty. It t-took me several y-years before I was allowed b-back here." He stared through the window.

"D-Did the p-police stop you c-coming home then, M-Mr Wrigley?" Jerry asked.

"No, I w-went into a m-mental hospital and t-they say it was the s-shock that left me w-with this s-stammer. A-Anyway, I thought if it wasn't for that b-bloody thing, it would n-never have h-happened and I would still h-have my dear Jenny and little Amy."

"How do you know it was that what did it?" Jerry asked Mr Wrigley.

"W-Well, if I had not been down there with that b-bloody thing, I would have been d-doing something else c-closer to the house. Anyway w-when I returned, I tried to d-dig that b-bloody thing out of the ground with my t-tractor, but every time I tried, the t-tractor just died on m-me. I tried to dig it out b-but every time that n-noise got so loud in my head I p-passed out.

"B-But one day, however, I was s-starting to dig when I h-heard a voice. It seemed to come from heaven. There was a s-sound like a h-heavenly choir and a b-beam of b-bright light, or a bright g-glow coming from somewhere. It was very s-strange. I could see a f-figure like an angel in the g-glow and a voice s-said that one day I w-would be with Jenny and Amy again.

"A w-warm feeling came over m-me and I knew s-something would guide me too them. And, I t-think, you are it boys?"

"God, that's given me goosebumps, Mr Wrigley. But why has it let us find it?" Johnny said.

"I don't kn-now but it has. It may h-have known that I w-wanted to destroy it and b-blamed it for the death of My Jen, or p-perhaps it knows you can get s-something it needs. W-Well, w-whatever it is, I'll help if I can." Mr Wrigley said.

"Hey, it did tell us to come back with it, Johnny."

"With what?" Mr Wrigley replied looking a little confused.

"I don't know, it didn't say."

"C-Come on let's go and have a look at w-what you found." Mr Wrigley said, putting on his wellington boots.

They got ready and made their way across the field on Mr Wrigley's old tractor. As they arrived, something had happened to the whole site. The hole had gone. It was as though no one had been there at all. Not even a footprint in the ground. This was stupid, how could this be? They tried their metal detectors to find the opening: nothing. Nothing at all.

"This d-doesn't make any s-sense at all it w-was here, I kn-now it was." Jerry said.

"D-Don't worry, it is here and it w-will let you f-find it

again w-when it's ready. Are y-you thinking the s-same as me? It's not f-from this p-planet?" Mr Wrigley said.

"That thought had crossed my mind. Well, I suppose we better get off home, if that's OK with you, Mr Wrigley?"

"Y-Yes, there isn't a lot you c-can do now, but you m-must keep in touch," said Mr Wrigley.

"Oh yes, we will, as soon as we can sort things out we will get back to you." They got on the tractor and made their way back to the farmhouse.

"C-Come on, let me r-run you into town." Mr Wrigley said, walking to his Land Rover.

"That's very kind of you and that would be very nice, Mr Wrigley. Do you mind if we leave our detectors here?" Johnny asked.

"Y-Yes, that will be OK and at l-least I know you'll c-come back to see me. I d-do get a bit lonely at t-times." Mr Wrigley said.

They got their things together and made their way to the Land Rover, put them in the back and got in. Mr Wrigley drove them down to the town.

"W-Whereabouts do you live l-lads?" he asked as he got close to the edge of town.

"J-Just down here n-near that b-bus stop will be fine, w-we only live over there." Jerry said.

"This is s-stupid, I might as w-well take you home, it's n-not much f-further."

"That's kind of you, if you don't mind, take the next right." Johnny said.

He took the next right and dropped them off outside their homes. "D-Don't forget w-what I've t-told you, if you n-need any help I'll t-try and give it." Mr Wrigley said.

After reaching their street, Mr Wrigley said it felt like a lead weight had been lifted from him and he could tell that some good was going to come from this. They all waved to each other and said again that they would keep in touch. Mr Wrigley drove off and made his way back to his farm. Jerry and Johnny were still talking about their experience in the field.

"See you tomorrow for work."

"OK, don't let the bed bugs bite."

"Hang on a minute, we must make up a story about these bumps on our heads." Johnny said to Jerry before they went their separate ways.

"I had forgot about them, they hardly hurt any more."

"I know, we were walking under a bridge and some kids dropped a piece of wood on us. We tried to jump out of the way but it was too late and it hit us. We chased the little buggers but they got away." Johnny said.

"Yes, we tried to catch them but they ran to fast. Yes, that will do."

"Now, we have talked about it again, mine still hurts a little." Johnny said, feeling the bumps.

"Yeah, m-me to." Jerry replied, being a bit sympathetic.

So this was their story, and they stuck to it, word for word. They even told their parents and family.

The next morning, they got up for work. Johnny looked in the mirror, hoping the bumps had gone. But they had increased in size, but the redness had almost gone.

"Oh bugger, I look a sight." Johnny said to himself as he grabbed his coat, bag and packed lunch. He looked at himself in the hall mirror. "See you later!" he shouted as he left the house.

Johnny made his way down the road to call for Jerry. They usually walked to work every day. But for some reason he kept getting images in his head, he couldn't make out what they were. As he got closer to Jerry's house, he could see him stood on the doorstep waiting for him, which was very unusual. Jerry was never ready on time.

"Morning, Jerry. How do you feel today, I see your bumps are still there?" Johnny asked.

"Whacked, absolutely whacked. I didn't get much sleep, I kept seeing things in my mind. Then I had a nightmare about the skeleton and I keep seeing things."

"Like what?"

"I don't know they don't make any sense," replied Jerry.

"Me too, I thought these bumps would have been gone, and everything would be back to normal," Johnny said in a worried voice.

"Yeah. I d-ducked d-down under the m-mirror, and slowly came up, b-but they were s-still there." Jerry said, smiling.

"We're going to take some stick today, Jerry. I hope you're ready for it."

"N-Nothing could be as b-bad as Saturday." Jerry replied.

"Did it really happen, Jerry?" asked Johnny.

"It r-really happened and I'm w-wondering now w-what are we s-supposed to take b-back and when as it got to b-be back for?"

"Whatever it is, we must try and find it. It might be in the books at the library."

"M-Maybe, but w-what will it b-be about?" Jerry asked.

"Don't know, maybe flying through space, the solar system, the universe. Who knows?"

"You've b-been watching too m-much Star W-Wars and Star Trek."

"I know, we'll say we have a headache and get this afternoon off."

"Yeah, b-but I need the m-money."

"So do I, but we could get money by selling pictures of the

craft, if we play it crafty." Johnny said.

"That's a c-cracking idea, J-Johnny, if we c-can find it again," replied Jerry.

"OK, as soon as anyone asks about our heads, we say that some kids on the bridge threw something at us, we chased them but they were too fast, but we have a cracking headache."

"Neat. Hey, y-you can see S-Sarah." Jerry said, joking.

"Jerry, if you want to live the day out don't say anything about Sarah, OK?"

"OK, y-you're t-touchy today, J-Johnny boy."

"Sorry, Jerry. I'm still a bit shaken by yesterday I think."

"Yeah, me too. I still don't know what happened, but looking at these bumps, it sure did."

On arriving at work, it didn't take long before the teasing started. And straight away there were a lot of comments about their bumps on their heads.

"God, what have you two been up to now?" one of the men shouted across the courtyard.

"Bumped your heady-wedys did we? You look like Humpty Bumpty!" shouted another, laughing.

"No, they tied their shoelaces together and tripped up, chasing Sarah square-eyes again."

"Go stick your head up your ass." Johnny said in an angry voice.

"Hey, Tarzan, we could always settle this at lunchtime," shouted the first man.

"C-Come on, Johnny, we're in enough t-trouble as it is. L-let's leave it." Jerry said, trying to calm the situation.

They took a load of stick, but went inside the factory and got on with their work, still talking about what had happened over the weekend. They wanted to keep it a secret. And anyway, who would believe such a story?

57

CHAPTER 3

The Powers

It was lunch time at the factory and the pair were in the canteen, looking through the window at the rain, making patterns on the windows while eating their sandwiches. The gaffer came in and walked straight across to them. Someone had told him that they had bumped their heads and that it had happened at work. He was worried because someone said they were going to the union about safety in the factory and he didn't want that because it could close his factory if health and safety got involved.

"What the hell have you two been up to?" asked Mr Bagshaw, in a sympathetic voice.

"Some kids lobbed a stick at them," a chap shouted on the next table.

"Yeah, they thought they were a couple of dogs fetch Rover," laughed another.

"Very bloody funny." Mr Bagshaw said, turning around to the table behind him. "You better get to the nurse and let her have a look at that, then, get your dinners and go straight to her. So, you didn't do it at work then?" he asked, not so worried now.

"No, it happened on Saturday."

"Right, right, make sure you see the nurse before you do anything else." Mr Bagshaw said.

After lunch, they got up and all the people in the canteen

stopped eating and looked at them. They smiled at them and made their way to the medical room and knocked on the door.

"Yes!" came a sharp, rough voice.

Jerry pushed Johnny towards the door. "G-Go on then, g-go in, she won't bite." Jerry said.

"Don't know about that, she sounds a bit nasty to me."

Johnny opened the door.

"We h-have b-been s-sent b-by Mr Bagshaw."

"What the hell have you two been up to?" the nurse asked.

Again, they told her the same story about the boys throwing things at them from the bridge. After a closer inspection, she said they should go to the hospital and let them have a look at the bumps. That afternoon, they were taken in the firm's van and dropped off outside the hospital.

As the two sat in the hospital waiting room, there had been a very bad accident involving a minibus of school children and a lorry. Over the loudspeaker came a message that there could be a two-hour waiting time due to the accident. Some of the patients were getting very restless, some of them had been waiting two hours or more already.

It wasn't long before the first of the casualties came into the hospital. The first child that was brought in had one ambulance man pushing the trolley and the other was applying pressure to the young girl's leg, but as they manoeuvred the trolley through the doors, an ambulance man turned round and accidentally released the pressure. Oh my God, blood gushed from a large wound on her leg.

An ambulance person shouted to a nurse, "It's an arterial bleed, get me someone, quick!" The nurse, already seeing to other patients, pointed to Johnny.

"Can you come and press on this padding hard, please. We

need help here," she shouted.

Johnny got up without even questioning her instructions and applied pressure to the large cut. Suddenly, a faint sound of what could only be described as a choir singing could be heard in the whole waiting room. A purple-blue glow started to appear under his hand, which was becoming very hot. He pulled away from the girl and wondered what was happening. There was a great deal of heat and Johnny sank to the floor.

The nurse rushed back to the girl who is now sitting up on the trolley.

"Thank you, young man, are you all right?" she asked in a concerned voice. "No dear, lie down, until I can get a doctor to have look at your leg," she said.

"You're s-some use, Johnny fainting at the s-sight of blood." Jerry said, taking the mickey.

"It wasn't that. I just got hot and all my strength seemed to go for a minute."

The nurse looked down at the leg to find a hairline scar over the area where, a few minutes ago, blood had been gushing.

"What the hell? Am I cracking up or what?" the nurse said out loud.

Jerry got up and helped Johnny back to his seat. Another nurse came in and was followed by a doctor.

"How did you do that, Johnny?" Jerry asked.

"I don't know. I was just touching her and this warm feeling come over me and I could feel that something was happening between us. It was as though I was closing her skin. It was very strange. God, I feel so hot in here, I hate hospitals," Johnny replied.

"Come here and let me feel your temperature, young man.

Perhaps I could be a doctor." Johnny said, laughing.

Johnny reached forwards and touched Jerry's forehead, which to his surprise was very hot. He then touched the back of his hand, again the singing noise could be heard Jerry pulled away from Johnny very quickly.

"You can pack that in, God I'm hot enough without you making me more nervous." Jerry said.

"Hey, you are really hot, Jerry perhaps it's a good idea to see a doctor." Johnny said, a little concerned.

"Bloody hell, Jerry, what's in your hand?" Johnny asked.

"Nothing, nothing. You got that same feeling didn't you?" Jerry opened his hand.

"Yes, it was like we were one, but I can't explain what I mean," said Jerry.

"Yes, but what does it mean?" Johnny said, confused.

"I don't know, but my throat feels like I've a warm towel around it and I have a tickling feeling." Jerry said, starting to cough. "God, it's getting so warm in here."

"Are you OK?"

"Yes, I'll be OK. I could do with a cold drink." Jerry replied.

"Jerry, you didn't stutter. What the hell is happening?"

"Don't ask me." Jerry said in a very surprised voice.

The nurse came across to them. "What did you do to that girl?" she asked.

"Nothing, I just helped."

"You did something because she was bleeding very heavily from a large wound and now there is hardly a scratch," she said, tapping her foot.

"I didn't do anything, honest. I just did what you asked me to do and that's all."

Over the loudspeaker, a voice said. "Mr Smith and Mr Henshaw please come to the reception." They got up and made their way to the counter.

"Have you both come to see Dr Jepson?" asked the nurse.

"Yes, if that's who looks after Mr Bagshaw's factory," Johnny replied.

"What is it in connection to?" she asked.

"We bumped our heads and these two lumps have appeared." Johnny said, pointing to the lumps.

"Take a seat over there and he will come to you," she replied.

About fifteen minutes passed and finally a doctor came to them.

"Mr Smith and Mr Henshaw?" the doctor asked. "Come with me please," said the doctor, opening the door to his surgery.

They went in and were told to take a seat. The doctor asked them questions about how long ago was it since this happened, and how did it happen, etc.

"You both seem to be all right but, to be on the safe side, I will send you for X-rays," he said.

"How long will we have to wait for that. We have been here for ages now." Jerry asked.

"Shouldn't be too long now, we have got on top of the emergency. In fact, if you go with that nurse, she will take you up to the X-ray department right now."

The doctor called the nurse over and was told to take them for an X-ray as soon as possible as they had been here quite some time. She took them upstairs. They both waited outside a small room for their X-rays to be taken. They were seated in the corner where a little boy was also sat with his mother. It looked like he had hurt his arm as it was in a sling and, with what looked like, a bad break in his arm. He seemed to be very distressed and in a great deal of pain. Johnny took out a pen from his top pocket and drew two eyes on the side of his index finger. He closed the finger around the back of his thumb and drew a mouth across his thumb and finger, making it look like a small face.

"Hello," he said to the little boy, opening his thumb to make it like the little puppet face was talking to him.

The little boy turned away.

"I'm sorry. He's not a happy chap. He's broken his arm and we are waiting for some more X-rays, then the surgeon will take a look at him. They think he will need an operation to correct it," said the little boy's mother.

"Oh, I am sorry; can I kiss it better for you?" Johnny asked again through the small puppet face on his hand.

The little boy nodded and a little tear rolled down his face.

Johnny gently held the boy's hand and, with his puppet, kissed the area that was broken. The same choir-like voices became audible and the purple-blue glow came between them both. The boy eased up off his mother's knee.

"Steady," she said to Johnny.

"Mummy, my arm. It doesn't hurt any more."

"Well, that must have been some magic kiss sweetheart. Sit still while we wait for the doctor. He won't be long."

A nurse came out of the room and asked for Jerry Henshaw. Jerry got up and went into the room. When he returned a few minutes later, it was Johnny's turn. They were told to wait downstairs and the doctor would see them.

In the A&E waiting room, they were still dealing with the coach crash victims. In a cubical was the driver of the minibus.

The curtains opened and a doctor came out. They heard him say more than likely it was a heart attack. They both stood there, their eyes staring forwards, to see a bright beam of light shine down. A beautiful heavenly body appeared in the fog-like mist, its arms reaching out for the dead driver. A mist rose from the driver's body and floated towards the figure. The apparition looked across at Jerry and Johnny and smiled at them as though it knew them. They looked at each other in disbelief.

"Shit, this is getting weird, do you think we should get out of here?" Johnny said, looking around the room to see who else had seen this happen. No one had seen any of it they all just sat there, oblivious to anything.

Just then a nurse called them both in to see the doctor.

"Well, I've had a look at your X-rays and they seem to be fine, except for this little patch. It could be an error because you both have it in the same place. Other than that, you are free to go. We will take a closer look at these X-rays and will contact you if we want to see you again. If you have any more problems, please come back and we will look at you further."

They thanked the doctor and stood ready to leave. They opened the door when a nurse took hold of Jerry's arm.

"This is them!" the nurse from the A&E stood there with another doctor.

"We would like to talk to you two about that girl's leg, and the boy upstairs with the broken arm."

"I didn't do anything, I just sat there, honest." Jerry said.

"Great friend you are," replied Johnny.

"I don't care who did what, its how you did it," doctor said.

"I didn't do *anything*. I just touched them." Johnny said.

"Yes, I know that. The thing is, there is no indication of anything being wrong with them. Nothing at all."

"Can you tell me what's going on please?" asked the doctor.

"These two have touched two patients within a few minutes of each other. Both had quite bad injuries and now they are both cured. Nothing wrong with them, nothing at all," she told the doctor.

"Well, what have you to say about it?" asked the doctor.

"If we told you, you wouldn't believe us." Jerry was saying, but suddenly stopped and stared into the doctor's eyes. "What I will tell you is your daughter said it isn't your fault and not to worry, she will see you again and she is waiting with gramps."

"Don't try that with me, sonny. My daughter passed away—" said the doctor but was interrupted.

"June 23rd 1978. She died because the plug on the toaster wasn't fitted properly."

"How the hell do you know that?" asked the doctor.

"Easy. She told him. She's there by your side." Johnny said.

"If this is some sort of revenge or game, it isn't going to work and it's not funny," the doctor replied.

Jerry smiled at the doctor. "It wasn't your fault, Daddy," he said, but in a young girl's voice.

"Anyone can know that. It will take more than that to convince me, nice trick."

"Oh! Now you've done it! Gramps wants a word with you." Johnny said.

"I doubt that. He's been gone twenty-five years."

"He never knew it was you who dropped his gold pocket watch and set fire to his shed, but he said it was so hard when his little lady died, it just broke his heart. They would like you to know that they are in a safe place and are together and they are waiting for the day when you and grandma can all be together again."

A strange look came over Jerry's face.

"Doctor, Gramps is telling me, you will receive a call, grandma has just passed over." He stopped, looked to the side of the doctor as though he was looking into an open space and smiled. "She's here."

"You can stop this right now, you're mental," the doctor said.

"She has her hand on your shoulder, she said that the Lord's garden is a wonderful place, the light is so bright, it's a very happy place, and they are all together. Please don't be sad."

Just then, the doctors phone rang. The nurse answered.

"Dr Morgan, it's the Autumn Park Nursing Home," she said.

He walked across to his desk and took the phone from the nurse. "Hello, Dr Morgan."

"I'm afraid we have some bad news for you. Your mother passed away a few minutes ago. We're very sorry."

"Yes, I was afraid you were going to tell me that. I'll come as soon as possible."

He turned to Jerry. "How the hell did you know that? You're a sick bastard. Get out and don't come back!"

"But they told me." Jerry told him.

"Jerry, I told you we would get in trouble. Let's get out of here quickly." Johnny said, standing up ready to make a quick getaway.

"Trouble! I'll show you trouble! You pair of sickos," the doctor shouted while still in shock.

"We have powers, special powers, but we aren't allowed to tell anyone about them." Johnny said to Jerry as they made a quick dash for the exit.

"Nurse, send for the security, get them two removed," said the doctor, still in denial of what Jerry had just told him.

At the exit door to the hospital were two large, menacing-looking security guards.

"No, wait, get someone who is ill. We will show you." Johnny shouted, stopping quickly.

"And what about Psychic Sid? Where does he come into this?" asked the doctor.

"That's my power. I can, unfortunately, see the spirits of the people who have passed over." Johnny replied.

"Come with us and you'll see." Jerry said.

"OK, guards bring them, let's see what they can do," said the doctor. The two were marched out of the room and they were taken down along a corridor into a large ward. In the room were about ten patients all looking very ill.

"OK, start with Mrs Johnson. Tell me what's wrong with her, but don't you dare touch her," the doctor said.

Johnny started to walk across the room to Mrs Johnson, followed closely by both security guards.

"Not you, him," the doctor said to Jerry.

"He can't do it. He has been given a different power. We don't know why." Johnny said.

"OK, you go and take a look," he said to Johnny.

Johnny walked to the lady's bedside, placed his hand close to her and, after a few minutes, he said, "She has something wrong with her kidneys." He turned towards her and asked if he could place his hands on her. He looked up and closed his eyes. The same bright purple glow came from his hands, the heavenly music filled the room as he did it, he could see the infection in her kidneys and it was like he could see through her body.

"OK, you should be fine in a day or so." Johnny told her.

"Oh, so that's it? She's cured?" a second doctor who had come in the room to join them said.

"Should be," replied Johnny.

"OK, try Mrs Smedley over in that corner, she's been here for two weeks and we have just found out what her diagnosis is," the second doctor said.

They all walked into the corner of the room. There was a young woman laid in a steel frame.

"Yes, she has a back problem, but something we couldn't detect and she simply wasn't getting any better," the first doctor said.

Johnny did the same thing as before, the glow came in between his hand and Mrs Smedley. "She has a broken back, her spine is damaged." Johnny said.

"We already told you that," replied the doctor.

"I haven't finished. She also has a severe infection that is not allowing her spinal cord to repair." Johnny replied.

"How do you know that?" asked the doctor and looked somewhat puzzled at the other doctor and nurse.

"I feel it, as if it was in my body. I'm guided by someone up there," he pointed up to the ceiling and then turned to the girl.

"Do you mind if I try something. It won't hurt." Johnny asked and the young girl just nodded.

He placed his hands on her stomach and slowly went around her back. The same glow was there yet again, the sounds were also present. Everyone looked down in amazement as she started to move her feet, then her legs.

"Oh God, it hurts, please stop," she said but then suddenly relaxed and her head sank into the pillow.

Johnny closed his eyes tighter and, with his eyes shut tight, he turned his head upwards, as though looking up at the ceiling. His hands began to shake and the soft purple glow became an aurora around them, the heavenly sound filling the room again, like a choir singing but with a synthesiser tone. He gently removed his hands from her limp body and lowered her onto the bed, where she gave a sigh of relief.

"Well, that's it, you're OK. Now you can get up and walk." Johnny said, smiling.

"You just stay put young lady, don't listen to him. You still need physiotherapy before you can put any weight on those legs," the first doctor said.

"But I feel fine. My legs feel a little weak but I can feel my toes wiggle too. And look, I can bend my knees," she said, moving about when a few moments ago she was paralysed from the neck down.

She giggled as she waved her feet from side to side. She smiled and told him to come close to her bedside. As he did, she gave him a kiss on the cheek. Johnny blushed as it was the first girl that had given him a kiss, except his mum.

"May I thank you from the bottom of my heart? You are a miracle worker and I don't know who up there is helping you, but he sure knows his stuff. Thank you so much," she said with a tear of joy rolling down her face.

"I suppose it's God. There is no other answer, but I'm not a religious person and don't believe in things like that, so why he picked me I'll never know." Johnny said.

"Jesus Christ," a nurse said.

"That's what we said and he said searching." Jerry replied.

"Jerry, shut up. Let's get out of here." Johnny said, grabbing hold of Jerry's clothes.

"You certainly have a gift from somewhere. Can I touch your hand please?" said the nurse.

"Yes, if you want to." Johnny looked bemused.

"God bless you, both. You have been chosen and given a gift. Use it well. I will tell the Father about this miracle," she said, making the sign of the cross on her chest.

"Oh, please don't. We would like to keep it a secret for—" he suddenly stopped. He could see that the nurse had a tumour in her brain. So as not to make any more fuss, he placed his hand on her head. The purple glow came upon the nurse as Johnny placed his hand on her head.

"You have a very strong belief in your God and that's a very nice thing. But keep this a secret please." Johnny asked.

"I will do my best but a lot of people have seen what you can do and they are all talking about it," she replied.

"I hope we can come back one day and help everyone but for now we must go back to the ship and sort things out." Jerry said.

"Ship?" replied the nurse.

"Oh, the, err, Ship and Anchor pub." Johnny said, very quickly.

"That was quick." Jerry said with a smile.

"You're not from somewhere else are you?" she asked.

"Not us, just off the estate," they both said almost together.

The door opened and in came another nurse. "I'm afraid it's too late for that. The reporter from the local paper is outside and they want an interview with you," she said, looking through the round porthole in the ward door.

"No, no, we must go. We have so much to do. Is there a

back door we can use?" Johnny asked.

"Yes, follow me, but you must be quiet," she led them through a door and down some old stone steps into what looked like the basement. "This was the old mortuary. It has not been used for years."

Jerry looked around. "There are so many spirits in here that want to be set free, and they must be." He stood in the middle of the corridor and smiled. "I will help you," he said.

Jerry we don't have time for this."

"Sorry, Johnny but I have to do it. The craft is telling me to." Jerry replied.

"Oh, I can feel it now, we must do it." Johnny said, now standing with Jerry in the middle of the corridor.

They stood there as if they were talking to someone but the nurse couldn't see any one there. She looked at the two of them. "You're freaking me out, guys," said the nurse.

"Do not worry." Jerry said as he placed his hand into hers, "no one will harm you, these are just lost souls."

Tears filled her eyes as she could now see apparitions walking into a purple haze, a misty figure of a little girl turned, and walk up to the nurse.

"Are you my mummy?" said the little girl in a low, sad voice.

"No, sweetheart, she's waiting for you over there," the nurse said, wiping her eyes.

As she said this, the figure of a lady appeared, her arms spread out and a voice said, "Jessica, I'm here."

The little girl turned. "Mummy, where have you been all this time? I've missed you so much." The little figure walked towards the shape in the mist then, just as soon as it had appeared, the mist faded along with the voices.

71

"We can now leave, thank you for your help." Johnny said to the nurse.

"You will come back, won't you?" she asked.

"The Lord works in mysterious ways." Jerry said as they walked towards the outer door.

As they walked off down the passage leaving the nurse behind, Johnny looked at Jerry.

"The Lord works in mysterious ways? What the hell is that all about?"

"Well, she is very religious and if it makes her feel better, that's fine by me."

"You're getting too soppy," said Johnny.

They had a good look around. There was no one around so, with no more to do, they slowly and casually walked away.

CHAPTER 4

The Invention

They made their way back to the village and decided to visit the library, where Johnny was hoping to see Sarah again. When they arrived, they found it was Sarah's day off and she was studying at the college. After making enquiries, they went to the coffee machine and sat down.

The lady librarian came up to them and whispered, "And don't spill them like you did the last time you were in here, and make sure you drink them before you read a book, in fact, before you touch a book."

"If I had known Sarah wasn't on duty today, I wouldn't have come. I can't stand old grumpy guts. No wonder no one comes in here." Johnny said.

"What should we read then?" Jerry asked.

"I don't know. I fancy a science book or technology," replied Johnny.

"What, don't you do enough of that at work?" asked Jerry.

"Oh now you've gone and spoilt it." Johnny said.

"Now what have I done?" he replied.

"You said work."

They both sniggered.

"I'm going for a cowboy book or something with excitement." Jerry replied walking over to the non-fiction aisle.

While Johnny walked towards the science and technology

books and Jerry went to the non-fiction aisle. Jerry came back with his choice of book, and Johnny came back with a pile of books.

"How long do you think we're stopping here for? We only have an hour and three quarters." Jerry told him.

"I'll just have a quick look to see if there is anything of interest." Johnny said, opening the first book.

After a few minutes, he stopped and rubbed his eyes, looking in surprise at Jerry.

"What's up with you? Do you need glasses?" Jerry asked.

"Jerry, there's something not right."

"I know and I'm looking at it." Jerry said.

"No, look into your book."

"What do you mean?"

"Just look into it and squint your eyes."

Jerry did as he was told. He quickly pulled his head back.

"What's up, Jerry?"

"Shit, I've read that page. That would have taken five minutes. What's going on Johnny?"

"I don't know, but I've read five pages in less than a minute and I can remember every word."

Jerry turned the pages of his book and within minute, he had finished his book.

"I've got to get another book. I've read that one."

Johnny was in deep concentration with his book. Jerry got up but Johnny never even blinked.

"How you getting on, Johnny?" Johnny never looked up, it was as if the book had mesmerised him.

Jerry gave a frown and went to collect a new book. On his return to the table, he noticed Johnny was now going through the second book. And they weren't thin books either; they were very thick ones.

Johnny was deep in thought and was flicking through the pages like lightening. He closed the second book and started another.

"You've never finished them already?" Jerry asked.

"Yes, and it was very interesting. Did you know, if we used two 4635 integrated circuits and four 45k resistors and those new 50v 100uf surface mounted capacitors, we could lose almost a full circuit board?"

"No, that's very interesting," replied Jerry, who wasn't really interested. Johnny started his third book.

Jerry sat down with his new book and started to read. Once again, he squinted his eyes and read the whole page in a matter of seconds. He just flipped through the pages and within a couple of minutes, he had finished. Looking at Johnny flicking through his book, he thought might as well have a look at one of his books.

"Can I borrow one of those?"

"No, go and get your own!"

"OK, mardy arse, I'll get my own."

Jerry took his cowboy book back. He went to the science and technology books and picked books about Nikola Tesla and Albert Einstein. As he started to flick though the pages, he took the books, sat down and started to read them. He understood every word in the books. He couldn't believe how clever both these two men were, especially Tesla, I amount if inventions he came up with was unbelievable for all those years ago.

Johnny had almost finished five books, Jerry had completed four.

"Do you think we should get going?" Jerry asked.

"One more book. I think it's called the Science of Physics,"

Johnny replied.

Jerry had finished his book.

"I'll get it for you." Jerry said, as he stood up to take his books back.

He found the book, but also found one at the side of it, Our Solar System and Outer Galaxy. "Mmm," he thought to himself, "I'll have a quick read of that."

He took both books back to the table. By this time, Johnny had already finished the last book as Jerry passed him the book he had requested.

They both sat, glued to the books. Then a warning bell sounded to say the library was about to close and the old lady stood up at her desk.

"Anyone wishing to take a book out, please come now as we will be closing in a few minutes," she said in an authoritative voice.

They flipped through the papers in no time and took the books back to the shelves. They got their coats and walked to the door and said good night to the librarian.

"Good night boys... Oh by the way, I'll tell Sarah you were looking for her," she said, smiling.

Johnny bumped the glass door as he turned around with the shock of the comment from the old lady.

"Err, thank you," he replied, red-faced.

"Even she knows you fancy Sarah." Jerry said, teasing him.

They caught the bus home and made plans to meet up in the morning for their horrid day at work and the teasing they would get once again, but at least it was Friday and they could look forwards to the weekend.

They met up as usual and made their way to work. Back at work the following day, they both sat at their bench as usual waiting to see what was to be on today's roster. All they could think about was the unusual diagrams that kept appearing in their heads. It was like being tormented by the same dream over and over.

"God, I have a strange thought in my head. Last night, I was in the ship and it showed me an electronics diagram and I was told to build it as soon as possible and return with it." Jerry said.

"That's unreal. I had the same thoughts. Look, I'll show you." Johnny replied. He picked up a piece of paper and started to make mathematical drawings as Jerry looked on. He was also adding to the drawings himself.

"The strange thing is Johnny, I can understand what I'm putting down on paper." Jerry said as he was adding items to the diagram.

"So do I, and I even know what components we need," he replied.

That day, Mr Bagshaw had to go to the doctors for blood tests because the factory nurse said his blood pressure was so high. "I'm off to the doctors for a check-up and blood test, my blood pressure is through the roof with you two messing me about," Mr Bagshaw said.

"Hope it's nothing serious, Mr Bagshaw. You should let Johnny give you the once over, he's good at that." Jerry told him.

"Not bloody likely. I wouldn't trust you two as far as I could throw you," he said, coughing as he was getting excited.

"Bye, hope everything is OK." Jerry said.

When Mr Bagshaw had left for the doctors, they sat at their bench and started to assemble the weird devices. They were full of the new integrated circuits that had just been invented, along with new, and much smaller resistors, and capacitors. Once they were finished they hid them under their bench until later, in the hope they could try them out before returning it to the craft.

"I wonder what it does." Johnny said, turning the circuit board around looking at it from all angles.

"I don't know but these wires need connecting to a power supply. Should we try it?" Jerry said excitedly.

"Let's try it," they both said at the same time, smiling at each other.

"We could ask Mr Bagshaw if we could stay over and lock up for him and, if so, when everyone has gone home, we could try it out." Johnny said.

"I can't see him trusting us with the keys."

"I'll see what he says and see if we can stay behind and finish."

"He'll not fall for that."

"He will, you know. Remember what he said, this order must be ready." Johnny said, winking at Jerry.

So, later that evening Johnny approached Mr Bagshaw on his returned from hospital.

"Excuse me, Mr Bagshaw, would it be OK if we stopped and finished the last four computer projects. We could lock up for you and bring the keys round to your house." Johnny asked.

Mr Bagshaw was gobsmacked. "Are you feeling OK? You can't wait to get out of here," he said.

"Well, we feel a bit sorry that we have made you ill. We thought it was only right that we finished today's work off."

"I'll tell you what, me and the missus are off out to celebrate her birthday so I'll come back and lock up, that should give you a couple of hours. How's that sound?" he said, still feeling a little uncertain.

"OK, we should be finished by then. I hope you're feeling better soon." Johnny said in a sympathetic voice.

They had worked for hours without stopping and by using Mr Bagshaw's factory, and staying to do the overtime for free, they finally finish Mr Bagshaw's work. And after several hours they had built the circuit board, full of the components they had seen in their dreams; and they were ready for the return to the craft.

Once Mr Bagshaw had left the building, they pulled out the device they had constructed and plugged in several wires into the electric sockets. A faint humming sound could be heard, with a lime-green glow starting to appear around the circuit. Their hair started to stand up and pens and paper started to roll towards it. The clock on the wall started to go backwards, the lights went bright and then faded to almost off, they then went really bright and started to explode. Pop! Pop! Then their work bench started to rise off the floor.

"Shit! Jerry, turn it off. What the hell is this?" Johnny shouted.

"I don't know, but it sure works good." Jerry replied as he pulled out the wires from the main socket.

"OK, let's start the other one and we will take them back to the ship."

"Yes, that's if it lets us back in, I wonder how Mr Wrigley's getting on. I feel very sorry for him knowing what happened to his wife and kid." Jerry said.

"Yeah, he's a nice old chap. Funny that I was thinking about him too. We must phone him." Johnny replied.

Plugging in the second device it, too, started to make a humming noise with a purple glow coming from it.

"Shit." Jerry said as they watched the two devices join

together to form one unit.

"I didn't do that, Johnny. I think we are a getting out of our depth you know."

"Look, there must be a reason why we had to build this, so let's get it home and we can take it up to the farm at the weekend."

They waited for Mr Bagshaw to come and lock up the factory and made their way home.

"Who's going to keep it?" Jerry asked.

"I can take it. We have a spare room and it's full of junk. No one goes in there. It will be safe till tomorrow." Johnny replied.

"If I took it home, Mam would be asking all sorts of questions." Jerry replied.

"OK, so what time do you want to go up to see Mr Wrigley then?"

"Whenever you like. But not too early, me mam likes a lie in."

"What about eight? That should get us there round about nine to nine thirty."

"Yeah, that should be OK," replied Jerry.

Johnny took the device and placed it inside his jacket. As they walked down the alleyway back to their homes. "Jerry, this thing is getting quite warm," he said, opening his coat.

"Yeah and its bloody glowing too. Put it away before someone sees it."

They split up and made their way to their homes. Johnny got home and went in.

"You're late. Where you bin? Ya dinner's on the table, I'll warm it up in the microwave for ya."

"OK, Mam, just going to the toilet." Johnny said, making

his way upstairs to the spare room. He placed the device in the corner and covered it with a old blanket.

He washed his hands and while he was drying them he took a look in the mirror. "God, I'm sure these bloody bumps are getting bigger," he thought to himself.

He made his way back down to the dining room, pulled his chair out and sat down waiting for his mam to serve him is dinner.

"Here and be careful it will be very hot. Anyway, what you been up to with that Jerry boy?"

"What you mean?"

"Well, there has been a reporter here, something about the hospital. It was all gobbledygook to me. I said you must have the wrong house and shut the door," she said.

"Search me. I ain't even been to the hospital." Johnny said making out it was a surprise.

"Well, I don't know about that, but you should go to Doctor Tate's and let him have look at those bumps on your head. I'm sure there getting bigger," she replied, pouring up a cup of tea.

After dinner, Johnny went up to his room. He had a peep in the spare room, just to make sure the device was OK. But as he opened the door, he was in for a big shock. Everything was floating around the room and the device had the light green glow around it again.

"*Johnny!*" came a loud shout from his mam downstairs.

"Yes, Mam?" he replied.

"Have you done something to the electricity? The lights are flickering and the telly's gone off. No, it's come back on again," she said.

"No, Mam. It must be a power cut or something," Johnny said, taking hold of the device and taking it into his room.

The device stopped glowing and Johnny placed it under his bed sheets and lay by the side of it. He must have been tired as he fell fast asleep.

The next morning he woke and looked at the clock. "Eight o'clock. I better get up and go for Jerry," he thought out loud.

He got dressed then went downstairs. After breakfast, he told his mam he was going out and would be back for tea.

He got his coat, went up to his room and got the device and made his way to Jerry's house.

Johnny called around for Jerry who was waiting on the door step. "You said eight, it's now like eight thirty." Jerry said, a little disappointed.

"Well it's the first time you've been ready." Johnny said, getting his own back.

"Hey, what do you reckon, me mam said we had a reporter from the *Gazette* asking if he could have a talk to me. She said, 'No, bugger off, he's done nothing wrong." Jerry said, laughing.

"When me mam's got it on her she can be nasty."

"Yeah, don't I know it!" Johnny replied.

"Have you got the you-know-what?"

"What?"

"You know, *it*?"

"It. Of course I have it. And I should have let you have it. The lights went out then on again, the telly went off and on, me mam went bonkers. She was watching her soaps. What a bloody night I had. And then, to top it all off, I went in the spare room where I put it and everything was floating around the room. It shit me up, I can tell you. I'll be pleased to see the back of it. Come on, let's get going or we will miss the bus. And the next one will be about another hour." They made their way to the bus stop, with Johnny trying to hold the device up inside his coat with both hands.

"I think this is getting heavier, Jerry?" Johnny said, hitching the device up higher in his coat.

"Well, you can sit down while we wait for the bus." Jerry said as they turned the corner at the top of the road for the bus. "No you can't, it's here!"

They now had to run to catch it and they got there just in time.

"You'll have to pay, Jerry. I can't take my hands out."

"Oh OK. Two to Wrigley Farm please," Jerry told the driver.

"Didn't you two go there last week? Christ, what you been up to, they're a pair of crackers," the bus driver said, pointing to the bumps on their heads.

"Accident at work." Johnny said, rushing to take a seat.

"You want to make a claim for that," the driver replied.

Jerry paid the driver, they smiled and made their way to their seats and sat down.

"Jerry, this is getting warm again." Johnny said, wriggling about.

The bus started to move then it stopped.

"What the hell is up with you?" the driver said to the bus. He was just about to get out of his seat when the engine started up again. "That's all I need, a bloody breakdown," the driver said.

With a few jerks, the bus lurched forwards and made its way up the hill. It didn't seem to take long and Wrigley's Farm was soon in sight. "Wrigley's Farm!" shouted the driver.

The two got up thanked the driver and made their way to the farm.

The big gates were open and there was no sign of Mr

Wrigley. "Do you think he's gone out?" Jerry asked.

"Don't know," replied Johnny.

Just then, a tractor could be heard coming down the road. Mr Wrigley pulled into the farmyard.

"W-well b-bless my s-soul, the w-wonderers return. And h-how happy I am to see you. C-come inside and we w-will have a c-cuppa." He got down from the tractor and led them into the house. "N-now then, t-tell me everything."

"First things first, sit down here, Mr Wrigley." Johnny said.

"W-whatever for? L-let me put the k-kettle on f-first," he said, putting the kettle on the stove. He turned and sat down in the chair. "N-now w-what?"

Johnny stood behind him. "I just want to put my hands on the back of your neck." Johnny said, placing his hands gently on Mr Wrigley's neck.

"Y-you not going to s-strangle me are y-you?" he said, laughing.

"No, but it will tingle a little." Johnny replied.

He placed his hands on Mr Wrigley's neck. The purple haze appeared again.

"What's going on? Is this a prank or something? My throats hitching from the inside out. Can you stop it, please?" Mr Wrigley asked.

"There, that should have sorted it, say something." Johnny instructed Mr Wrigley.

"What you on about? I haven't shut up since you came." Mr Wrigley replied.

"Mr Wrigley, say something and listen to what you're saying."

"Like what? And what you on about?" he said, confused.

"You're not stuttering any more." Jerry said.

"Well, what do you know. How did you learn that trick lad?" Mr Wrigley said in amazement.

"Don't know. I just seem to put my hands on people and can repair what's wrong. Ever since I came out of that thing in the field last week." Johnny said just as confused as the others.

"*And*, it told us to make this." Jerry said, pulling the device out from under his coat.

"What the heck is that contraption?"

"That is what we would like to know." Johnny said.

"Well," said Mr Wrigley, "we'll have this cuppa and a slice of cake and make our way down to that thing. We can go on the tractor."

After their refreshments, Mr Wrigley went into another room and came back with their metal detectors. "We better take these with us or you will never find it. I've been down there a few times and it looks like no one has ever been digging there, never mind uncovered anything," he said, holding the detectors up.

So, picking up the device and the detectors, they put on their coats and made their way to the tractor.

"What about the spades?" asked Jerry.

"Spades? I'll just dig it out with the tractor. It won't take long with that."

They boarded the tractor and made their way down the field to the hump that could just be seen from the height of the tractor. As they got closer, a rumbling sound could be heard and the ground began to shake.

"What's going on?" Mr Wrigley asked.

"I think it knows we are on our way." Johnny said. Sure enough, as they got closer to the object, there in front of them was the metal object shining in the sunlight.

"That can't be. I was only down here yesterday and there was nothing here."

"Well, there is now, so we don't need the tractor or the detectors."

They got out of the tractor and slowly made their way towards the object. A warm feeling came upon them. "For some reason, I feel very happy." Jerry said, smiling.

"Me too," replied Johnny.

"I don't know what you mean but I do feel something strange." Mr Wrigley replied.

As they walked towards the object, the doorway opened and the strange sounds could be heard again.

"Now this takes the biscuit. If I hadn't seen it myself, I would not have believed it." Mr Wrigley said, scratching his head.

"Come on, let's go in." Johnny said excitedly.

"I ain't going in there, it's pitch black." Mr Wrigley said, backing away from the entrance.

"It won't be, you'll see."

As they entered the object, the whole passageway lit up and it was much brighter than the last time they were inside. They made their way down the passage and entered the control room where the seats and the skeleton were.

"It's gone."

"What's gone? And why is it so big inside?" asked Mr Wrigley.

"You might not believe us but there was a skeleton in that chair. The air must have disintegrated the remains."

"This is amazing," said Mr Wrigley, looking all around the inside passageway. Once inside the control room, he was stunned by all the lights and monitors that had come on.

Suddenly, a thin vertical drawer opened. "Johnny, look here."

"I wonder if that's where this fits," replied Johnny, holding the device they had made.

He slowly placed the device into the slot in the drawer. It fit perfectly. The drawer slowly slid back into the unit.

"Take a seat." Jerry told Mr Wrigley.

"I think I'm dreaming. This, this thing, has been in my family's field for, well, I don't know how many years." Mr Wrigley said.

Then, like magic, there was a green glow from the drawer and a very low humming noise could be heard. "You have done well, bold travellers."

Mr Wrigley jumped and looked around in shock. "Who said that?"

"Oh, it's the, err, ship?" Johnny replied.

"I am now ready to find power, please commence with lift and search mode."

"What? What's it on about?"

"I think it wants its batteries charging up," replied Mr Wrigley.

CHAPTER 5

The First Flight

Now that the power pack had been installed, the craft configured all the memory banks and the navigation units were all modified. The craft could now start to recharge its power supply.

To do this, they would have to fly the craft over the national power grid lines and soak up the amount of power required for getting the ship into full working order. They were looking at the symbols, trying to work out which symbol did what. Jerry said, "I wonder what this one does," and pressed the button, several monitors lit up.

"You know what, I can understand a lot of the symbols but I am not sure which one is for lift off. Should I try this one?" he asked.

"I don't know. See what it does." Johnny replied, looking at the outside of the ship through the monitor.

"OK." Jerry replied as he pressed the button.

"Woo!" Johnny shouted.

"Look what you've done to me tractor." Mr Wrigley screamed. A laser had hit his tractor window screen and made a hole straight through it and out the side window and, if it hadn't hit the stone wall, heavens knows where it would have finished up.

"Sorry, should I give this one a go?" he asked.

"Well, take a guess. But *not the laser!*"

"This one looks a little like the one I saw in my dreams, but I'm not sure."

"Press it and see what happens. We can only blow up."

"Very funny." Jerry replied.

Jerry placed his hand over the symbol. A very faint hum could be heard and the ship gave a few vibrations and was slowly rising out of the ground. Johnny placed his hand on the monitor symbol. It was like the whole front wall of the ship had been removed and replaced by a large screen. There was a faint image appearing on the screen. It was a view of the outside but it looked like they were outside it was so clear.

"How the heck has that happened?" Johnny said.

Mr Wrigley was so confused, he went outside to see if the front of the ship had been removed.

"Hey up, look at Mr Wrigley. He's looking at us. Yo! Mr Wrigley!" Jerry said as he started to wave at him.

"Jerry, he can't see you."

"Oh yeah, I forgot, you know what, I'm going to ask him if he wants to come with us." Johnny said.

"OK captain, I'll put her down again." Jerry said now getting to grips with the controls.

Slowly, the craft lowered to the ground. Johnny got up and went to the entrance. He was about to place his hand over the coloured lights, when the door opened by itself.

"Hey, Jerry, this ship started to know what we want it to do before we do it." Johnny said as he climbed out of the craft and walked up to Mr Wrigley.

"Mr Wrigley, can you remember what we said when we first came here? About sharing everything three ways?" asked Johnny.

"I think so," replied Mr Wrigley.

"Well, we want you to come with us." Johnny replied.

"No, not likely. You don't know how to fly the bloody thing, he's smashed me tractor, he ain't even got a driving licence," he replied.

"OK, but once we learn how to control it, you'll come with us?"

"Yes, I suppose so, but now get going before someone sees you." Mr Wrigley said.

"OK, it's a deal! We will take it for a test run and come back for you." Johnny said, smiling.

"OK, it's a deal." Mr Wrigley said, thinking to himself there's no chance of this pair flying this thing.

Johnny ran back to the ship's doorway. He turned to Mr Wrigley. "I'll be back. Well I hope so," he said, entering the ship with the door closing behind him. He walked down the passage to the control room where Jerry was still watching Mr Wrigley on the huge monitor.

Mr Wrigley climbed into his tractor and put his finger through the hole in the windscreen that the laser had made. He started the tractor and drove clear of the mound of soil.

"Is Mr Wrigley coming back when he's moved the tractor?" Jerry asked.

"He didn't want to come. He said your driving was crap!" Johnny replied.

"Oh and you could do better, could you?" Jerry asked.

"Just joking. Come on, let's go. He said he would come with us the next time, once we had learned to fly it."

"Hey, look at this." Jerry said as he waved his hand over the controls. Again, the ship rose off the ground but this time it rose very smoothly. It was like the ship had connected to their thoughts.

"I could see everything outside the ship, with you and Mr Wrigley."

"Just look where you're going." Johnny told Jerry.

"Scotty to Captain, we can't take much more of this."

"Jerry, stop pratting about. We have been chosen to sort this craft out."

"OK, here we go." Jerry said.

The craft rose high into the night sky, slowly turning on its axis as it headed south and slowly started to move forwards.

"God, if this is the speed we are going to get out of this old jalopy, we might as well walk."

"Give it time. It's been buried for thousands of years."

"This is great, look at the view. Hey, look at that police car down there." Jerry said, pointing to the police car that was parked in a layby.

"Well, they won't get us for speeding, will they?" Johnny replied.

Just then, the ship turned towards the police car.

Jerry, what the hell are you doing?"

"Doing? I'm not *doing* anything. It's going crazy again."

"We're heading for that cop car. Pull up! Pull up!"

"I can't. It's not letting me. It's going to hit it!"

Down in the police car, the officer looked up into the night sky. To his amazement, there in front of him were several bright lights, heading towards him.

"Oscar hotel to central control, over," said the policeman.

"Receiving, over," came a reply.

"I have some weird lights in the skies above me, over," said the policeman.

"Can you repeat that please?" the reply came back.

The two looked at each other as they could hear the radio transmission from the police officer. "He's talking about us," Jerry said.

The craft hovered over the police car and started to drain the power from the car's battery. The car engine stopped and its headlights faded and went out. Inside the police car, the officer looked in amazement as his clipboard rose off the seat and his pen floated in mid-air. His radio had gone dead and all the lights had gone out. He looked out of the windscreen to see the underside of the huge disc hovering above him.

The officer now started to panic. "I said I want to report a UFO sighting. Hello? Hello? No, no, this is not happening to me. Oh, God, no one will believe me," he said, whacking the microphone on the dashboard.

The police car's lights came back on, but the engine wouldn't turn over or start due to the battery drain.

As the ship moved away from the car and towards a small housing estate, the lights of the houses directly under the ships path started to go out. It was acting like a vacuum cleaner, sucking every drop of energy from beneath its path. Slowly moving over the town, it was now heading towards the national grid power lines.

"I hope you're in control of this thing." Johnny said.

"Sure I am, it's a cinch." Jerry replied.

"Good because we're heading towards those pylons."

"Do you want a go?"

"No! Just miss the damn things," Johnny said, very excitedly.

As they got closer to the overhead cables, sheets of purple lightning started to float up from the cables to the ship. The lights on the whole housing estate and surrounding area started blinking on and off and suddenly went into a total blackout.

"Bloody hell, I hope we don't get hit by one of those lightning bolts."

"Hit by one? We're soaking it up like a sponge. It's after as much power as it can get."

Everything inside the craft came to life: lights, dials and monitors lit up. A faint humming sound from the motors could be heard as the power was now building up.

"OK, let's head south for the winter." Johnny said, joking.

The craft turned and headed south, Jerry waved his hand over the controls and the ship shot off at an unbelievable speed.

"Wow, now this is travelling, how fast do you think we are going?"

"Fast!" Jerry replied.

A couple of seconds passed and the lights on the control panel started to flash. The ships computer had now come into operation. "Shield from radar, you will be detected," came a voice from the computer. "Shield from radar, you will be detected," again the computer repeated itself.

"How do we do that?" Johnny asked.

"Would you like auto commands to be started?" asked the computer.

The ship slowed as if waiting for instructions and there in front of them, as they looked at the large screen, heading straight for them was a 747 jumbo jet. They were more surprised when they could hear the pilot's conversation with Heathrow Airport.

"Hotel foxtrot to Heathrow tower, I have a UFO in sight, can you confirm, over."

"Affirmative HF245, we have it on radar."

"HF to Heathrow tower, it is something saucer shaped and

heading straight for us."

"HF, that's affirmative, change heading to 356, altitude 31,000 feet, over."

"Hell! Shit! This is real! Descending to 31,000 feet," replied the pilot of HF245.

"Would you like auto commands to be started?" the computer voice said.

"Yes! Yes, do it, do it now." Jerry shouted in an excited voice.

"Confirm, do it, do it now." Johnny also shouted.

"Heathrow, the UFO is staying with us," the pilot reported.

The computer went into auto mode and put a device on that stopped them being picked up by the radar. But they were still heading straight for the 747 and the pilot could visually see the craft.

"We're still heading for it, can't you do anything?" Johnny shouted to Jerry.

The room started to glow a reddish purple, it looked like the ships computer had started to respond. "Now what's it doing?" Johnny shouted.

"Hostile alien craft approaching. Armed, suggest evasive action and destroy."

The main screen was now looking like a computer game. There were grid lines and what seemed to be a round circle with a cross in it, directly in front of them were two fighter aircraft, this was some sort of sight targeting on both planes. A radio signal was being received "This is Captain James of the RAF. You are in violation of British air space, please acknowledge, over."

"Shit! it's the air force. Computer, stop." Jerry commanded the craft.

The craft stopped dead. On the screen the two fighters were heading straight for them but the planes had to veer both sides of the ship.

"What do we do?" Jerry looked across at Johnny, somewhat scared of what might happen.

"Computer, do not fire, disarm and continue journey," he yelled.

It wasn't long before they were confronted by the flight leader, Captain Michael James. "I repeat, you are in violation of British air space, please answer, over."

"Oh bugger, Jerry, they'll shoot us down for sure." Johnny replied, almost screaming.

"Descent required," said the ship's voice.

"Yes, descend," he screeched almost losing his voice.

"Request distant distance," it asked.

"Err, down, quickly," Johnny screeched, but the ship did nothing. "Err, a thousand feet." The ship dropped like a stone to one thousand feet.

"Foxtrot one to foxtrot two. Did you see that? How the hell can it make a turn like that? Over."

"Beats me, over," replied foxtrot two.

"OK, let's follow my leader," commanded foxtrot one.

"Roger," foxtrot two replied.

They dived and turned at the same time and went down one thousand feet. The craft responded by dropping another ten thousand feet, again straight down at a ninety-degree angle. And again the fighters followed, but not at the same angle; they had to make a large descending sweep as the G-force would have knocked them unconscious. They started to gain on the craft. As they did, the ship's computer responded with, "It would be advisable to travel at impulse three. This will give you a greater distance from the approaching aliens?"

"Yes, do it." Jerry commanded.

It responded by moving away at incredible speed, well over two thousand miles per hour. This left the jets way behind.

"Foxtrot one to base, over."

"Base to foxtrot one, receiving, over."

"Foxtrot one to base. It's a waste of time. It can outrun us with every move, over."

"Base to foxtrot, you have permission to open fire, over."

Foxtrot one and two locked onto their target and set missiles for a direct hit.

The ship's computer advised them of a hostile attack and shields were advised.

"Yes. Bloody hell, shields," he said as he turned to Johnny. "They're going to shoot us down." Jerry said in panic.

He turned back to the screen. "Hey, we're bloody British, you plonkers."

"Fire at will." Captain James commanded.

They released a second missile at the craft. A green glow encased the ship and the missiles bounced straight off.

"Foxtrot one to base, nothing. Nothing happened. They bounced off."

"Can you confirm a direct hit, over?"

"Yes, but they just bounced off, over."

The ship's computer advised them to go into Earth's orbit and, without question, they did. The craft rose at an incredible speed and, within seconds, they were in orbit. Once in space, it was time to think what the best course of action would be.

"What the hell do we do now? We've got the air force after us, the police after us and were in deep shit." Jerry asked, looking out at the Earth far below.

"Perhaps it's time to get away from here." Johnny replied.

"You mean to the place where this ship came from?" asked Jerry.

"Or we could ask the ship what to do," he replied.

"Now hold on a minute, if you think I'm going to let some squidgy person-thing probing my bits and bobs, you've got another think coming." Johnny said in a concerned voice.

"There could be some nice lady aliens, you know." Jerry said, laughing.

"Oh yeah, as easy as flying to the Moon, I suppose."

"Affirmative, Earth's satellite planet 384,400 kilometres from Earth. Be seated. Five, four, three…" said the ships voice.

"What the hell, did *you*—" before Jerry could finish, the ship shot off so fast the Earth could be seen getting smaller by the minute.

"Forward scanners engaged," said the ship's voice.

The large screen came to life. In front of them on the screen was the image of the Moon coming closer and closer.

"Jerry, why can't you keep that big mouth of yours shut? Now look what you've done!" Johnny said.

"That's another fine mess you've gotten us into." Johnny said.

"You sound like Oliver Hardy." Jerry replied.

"Who?"

"You know, Laurel and Hardy."

"Very funny." Johnny replied, but was interrupted by the ship's voice.

"ETA to Earth's satellite, four point six Earth hours."

"Great! Satellite TV."

"It's talking about the Moon, you dickhead." Johnny replied.

97

"The journey to the Moon will take a few hours," Jerry turned to the monitors, "I wonder if we can get movies on this thing." Jerry said, looking at all the monitors.

"Christ, Jerry."

"Christ," came the ship's voice, after a long wait. "Searching," came from the ships voice. "His body was returned some 5,000 years ago. We had craft searching for him and that's when we crashed, due to power loss."

"What do you mean searching for him?"

"After we impregnated a human female, we tracked his progress. It was some thirty years later we lost track of him. We traced his body and it was recovered from a small hole in the Earth."

"Jerry, he's talking about Jesus." Johnny said.

"Do you mean Jesus Christ?"

"Affirmative," replied the ships voice. "Once he was destroyed we decided to stop the project and not visit Earth again."

"So were you planning to live here?"

"Some enjoyed Earth and were offered the chance to live among the humans. We have visited Earth again several times to monitor it, but we have found the humans have become so aggressive and unfriendly, we have never been back as we did before."

"So why have you waited till now to try and leave?"

"Earthlings didn't have the technology to make the small power packs that we asked you to make."

"So why did you stop people, humans, finding you in the past?"

"We tried to give the advice to make the power packs with several humans but none had the items to make the power packs. Some were very intelligent and, if the products had been available, they would have accomplished their task." Several images of people were shown on the monitors; several were noticeable: da vinci, Einstein and Tesla.

"Look, Johnny, I was reading about them in the library, I wondered why they were so interesting to me. How did you try and make them help you?"

We tried to implant thoughts while they were asleep like we did with you. We enter your brainwaves and use your subconscious to place thoughts of whatever we place there," the ship's voice said.

"Can you give us knowledge of what you wanted to achieve here in Earth?"

"What knowledge would you require?" asked the voice.

"This should be interesting." Johnny said.

"All knowledge." Jerry asked.

An image started to appear on the screen, it was the pyramids in Egypt. "You mean the pyramid?"

It looked like the ship was scanning the area around the pyramids. It stopped at the Great Pyramid.

"Why have you stopped here? Is this where the engine is?"

"Yes, it was left here in case one of us could not return."

"Christonions first visited Earth 15,000 years ago. Until 5,000 years ago, there was very little intelligence here. We then found that the Earth's gravitational pull was far too great for our engines to lift us after being in our hovering position for so long and then our ships' engines had insufficient power left to pull us clear into Earth's orbit. The mother ship that orbited the Earth encouraged the inhabitants of Earth to build round stone circles for us to land our ships on so we didn't have to use all our energy hovering for so many years and leaving the Earth before we returned to our planet."

"What sort of circles?" Johnny asked. An image came on the screen; it was Stonehenge. "You mean you got people to build these?"

"We got them to help. We found the rock and used our gravity instruments to lift and carry the heavy stones and erect them in place. There were several buildings all around this part of Earth."

"But what's the pyramids got to do with it?" Jerry asked the computer.

"Inside this pyramid," another image came onto the screen, "concealed is a chamber that contains the engine. It was buried so deep so not to injure any human. Just to be close to it would be fatal."

"But these have been searched by archaeologists for many years and they have only found mummies and items of treasure."

"Without the knowledge, it would be impossible to find the entrance to this chamber, never mind how to find the passage way," the voice said.

"So, I suppose we have to go and find the engine?" Johnny asked.

"You will. You will enter and you will find the way to the chamber and recover the power pack then return it to the ship," replied the voice.

"Just a minute, you said if you go near it you would be fried, or it would kill you." Jerry said.

"You will be protected with a suit."

"Oh, I think it's time we went home." Jerry said.

"When we go around the satellite, we will return to Earth," the ship replied.

The speed of the craft increased greatly. The Moon's surface could be seen very clearly. All the mountains and the craters could be seen in great detail. The craft flew very close to the surface and, when around the back of the Moon, down below, the boys could see what looked like derelict buildings.

"What are those? Buildings?" Jerry asked.

"We tried to use this satellite as a base, but due to the low temperatures and the energy required to keep this base, running it made it impossible, so we moved to Earth."

It only felt like a few minutes and the craft had gone round the back of the Moon and had started its journey back to Earth. Looking at the ships monitor, they could see the Earth, now looking like the Moon from Earth on a clear frosty night.

They looked in amazement as the craft got closer to the Earth and it was soon entering the Earth's atmosphere.

"Desired location?" the voice asked.

"Well, I don't know." Jerry replied.

"Err, back to your initial crash site." Johnny quickly said.

As the craft got closer, they could now see the coast line of Great Britain and, very quickly, the outlined hedgerows could be seen. The craft slowed and lowered into the field where it had been buried for many years.

"Oh my God, Johnny. We must go and tell Mr Wrigley about all this. He will be amazed by it all."

"He will! I can't believe it myself."

They left the craft and made their way to the farmhouse talking about the adventure they had just had.

Knocking on the door, there was no answer, so they knocked again. "Who the hell is it at this time of night, or should I say morning?"

"It's us, Mr Wrigley, Johnny and Jerry!"

There was a click of the lock and the door handle turned. A very sleepy-eyed Mr Wrigley peered through the slightly opened door. "Where the hell have you two been? We have had the police up here, the papers and God knows who else."

"What for?"

"They have been looking for a UFO. It's in the paper. They're calling it the 'Yorkshire Roswell'."

"What do you mean?"

"You have been gone almost two days. Where have you hidden it?" asked Mr Wrigley.

"Well, we have been to the Moon and we have to go to the pyramids."

"You better come in and tell me about it," he said. They sat down and Mr Wrigley put the kettle on. "Now slowdown and you can tell me about it."

They sat drinking their tea and started to tell the story about the police car and the power lines and nearly getting shot out of the sky. They were not sure if Mr Wrigley believed everything but he was very interested.

"Mr Wrigley, do you want to come with us tomorrow?" Johnny asked.

"Yes if you like," Mr Wrigley replied thinking they had made it all up. "Come on, you better get some rest and we will talk again tomorrow," Mr Wrigley said as he stood up and made his way to the stairs.

The following morning, they were up bright and early. They had made the fire and made breakfast before Mr Wrigley had come downstairs.

"Breakfast," they said as Mr Wrigley opened the door.

"So what are you two going to do today?"

"Well, we can't go to the craft till dark so we could help

around the farm."

"You're telling me what you said last night was true?"

"Well, yes." Johnny replied.

"So, you are going on a trip tonight?" he asked.

"Err, yes. And you're coming with us. There are three seats so you can be very comfortable."

"Now hold on, I thought you were kidding," he said.

"No, Mr Wrigley. We have to go to Egypt and the pyramids." Jerry explained.

"I think I have something to do tonight." Mr Wrigley replied.

"Come on, you can't chicken out now. You said if we learned to fly it, you would come with us. And you did agree to split with us whatever we found."

"Well, OK. But not to the bloody Moon, you promise?"

"OK, you can stay in the ship while we go and collect the power pack, I think it could be very dangerous. The computer or whatever, did say it could kill you without a suit on."

"Well, that's charming, you try and help and you might get killed. Lovely." Mr Wrigley replied.

They had been pottering about on the farm all day and had walked down to the field where the craft had landed. Looking over the wall, they were surprised to see the craft had buried itself into the ground.

They were getting excited about tonight's adventure, but Mr Wrigley was somewhat hesitant and not sure about this at all.

The night was slowly drawing in and the sun was setting. "Well Mr Wrigley, you ready for the trip?" Johnny asked.

"Not really. I'm still not sure about all of this," he replied.

"Don't worry, the ship won't let us get into trouble."

"It's OK, but them over there, their funny about them pyramids of theirs and if we get caught it will be…" Mr Wrigley said, pretending to throttle himself. "Come on, we'll have some tea and I suppose we will get going," he continued as he was putting the pots in the sink.

So, have tea they did. In fact, it was a very large tea. I think Mr Wrigley wanted it to last all night and hoped they would forget about going.

"Ready, Mr Wrigley?" Jerry asked putting on his coat.

"I suppose," he said, thinking, "what have I let myself in for?"

"Come on Mr Wrigley, you look like you don't want to come. Where's your sense of adventure?" Johnny asked.

"I think it went about two hours ago," he replied.

They all put on their coats and boots and made their way to the ship. Reaching the stone wall, they could see the top of the ship. Mr Wrigley was becoming very agitated. "Do you think this is a good idea boys?" he asked.

"Look, if these built the pyramids then surely they have the right to go inside."

"Yeah, that's what I'm worried about," he said.

"Come on, it will be OK. We have seen what this ship can do and it's only running on about half power." Jerry said.

They went over the stile in the wall and made their way to the ship. As they approached, the doorway opened. Well, it didn't actually open it seemed to melt.

"Look lads, I'm not too sure about this you know." Mr Wrigley said very nervously.

"Oh, get inside, it'll be fine." Jerry replied.

So, very gingerly, they entered the craft and made their way into the control room. Mr Wrigley was shown to a seat.

"Hey! This ain't where that dead body was, is it?" he asked.

"No," Johnny replied, winking at Jerry. "Anyway, he just turned to dust. It was the oxygen entering the ship and it just went to powder," he continued.

"What did he look like anyway?"

"Computer can you show an image of Christonions?" Johnny asked the ship's computer. The large monitor came to life and a image of Christonions was displayed. It was so life like.

"Oh, I'm sorry I asked." Mr Wrigley said, pushing himself into his seat.

Mr Wrigley was now feeling more settled and looked like he was waiting in anticipation of the flight to commence. The two men sat in their seats and the ship came to life.

"Ready for flight... heading for the... Pyramids," said the ship's voice.

"OK, start flight." Johnny commanded.

The ship slowly rose up into the night sky and hovered for a while above the trees. It started to rotate in the direction of the pyramids. Within a second the ship had accelerated to an unbelievable speed.

"Blimey, this is faster than the old tractor!" Mr Wrigley said with excitement.

Within minutes, the coast line of the Mediterranean Sea could be seen approaching. The ship slowed and raised high above the Egyptian coast line. There, in front of them, could be seen the pyramids. The ship made its way towards the Great Pyramid.

"What are we looking for?" Johnny asked.

An image appeared on the screen.

"Hell, that's The Ark of the Covenant?" he said.

"This is the power source we require, we are approaching the encasement?" the ship's voice replied.

"I've seen that in films. It melts people." Jerry said.

The ship hovered over the Great Pyramid.

"What if we are seen?" asked Mr Wrigley.

But there in front of them, a whole section of the side of the pyramid pushed forwards and started to part. The craft slowly made its way towards the opening. Once inside, the opening closed behind them.

"This is unreal. We are actually inside the pyramid."

The craft lowered and hovered at ground level and the doorway opened. In front of them was a long passageway. Inside the ship, a panel opened and three suits on hangers came out.

"Please put the suits on and follow these signs. A hieroglyphic symbol comes on the screen. "Remember this, it will be required," the voice said.

"I'm not going in there." Mr Wrigley said very nervously.

"Well, you can stay here, but you must put the suit on, for when we come back with the power pack, it will kill you," Johnny said.

"What have you got me into? I'm not too happy about this." Mr Wrigley said.

"You'll be fine, just don't touch anything."

They put on the suits, Jerry slipped into his very easily. Johnny and Mr Wrigley's suit was somewhat snug.

Once they had their suits on, three head pieces lowered from a ceiling compartment.

"Make sure these are airtight," the voice requested.

They helped each other to put on the helmets and make

sure that they fit properly.

"OK, they're on." Johnny said.

"Testing," said the ships voice as a light purple mist entered the control room. "Monitoring," it said again.

After a few minutes, the mist vanished as quickly as it had come into the control room. "You are now in your own atmosphere. Do not remove the helmets, suits or the gloves," it said.

In front of them, a small shelf slid out of the wall. There was a fluorescent orange pad fixed on the top. "You will require these," the voice said.

"What will they do?" Johnny asked.

"The one on the left will show you the way. The other will encase the unit and allow you to release the gravitational pull for you to bring the power pack back to the ship," replied the voice.

They took one of the devices each and held it in their hand.

"This is like a satnav map. Look, it's showing us the passageways." Jerry said excitedly.

"I feel like a goldfish in a glass bowl." Mr Wrigley complained, and fidgeting around on his seat.

"Look, just sit there and don't move. *And* don't touch anything!" Johnny commanded as he opened the outer door.

"I knew I should have stayed at the farm." Mr Wrigley muttered to himself.

The two boys slowly made their way to the outer door and into the passageway. Instantly, the device Jerry was holding lit up, making some of the stones in the passageway walls light up like street lights but there was no visible light source.

They very slowly made their way to what looked like a dead end. There was a solid stone wall.

"Now what?" Jerry said.

Just then a beam of light came from the device Jerry was holding. It shone onto a stone on the side panel. The image of the four hieroglyphic symbols appeared on the wall.

"Go on then, touch it." Johnny told him.

"Oh yeah, I've seen these things on movies. You touch them and something shit happens." Jerry replied, being very reluctant to touch the symbol.

Jerry slowly raised his hand and placed it on the symbol the computer had shown them. A faint rumble could be heard and, like magic, the stone wall was no longer there. It was like someone had just used a rubber on a drawing and rubbed out the wall.

"Come on." Johnny said in a very excited voice as they entered into the next passageway.

In this passage was a sharp left turn to yet another blank wall. There were more hieroglyphic symbols that appeared again. Jerry placed his hand on right one and the wall parted leading them into a very small room.

"Now what? There is nothing in here." Jerry said.

Suddenly, the stone wall closed behind them. "I told you something would happen. Oh God, we will be in here forever," he said almost in tears.

Then, with a sudden jolt, the floor seemed to drop.

"Jerry, it's a lift. We are going down." Johnny said in worried voice.

"This is your fault. I never wanted to go to that bloody field in the first place." Jerry replied now becoming a little hysterical.

The lift came to a stop and the wall again parted. The room was glowing; it was almost as bright as the sun. The visors on the helmets polarised, which brought down the brightness of the room. There in front of them was the power plant. To their amazement, this is where the bright light was coming from. The Ark of the Covenant. There were the sounds of what can only be described as a heavenly choir.

"Jerry, that's the sound that happens when you touch people."

"It's coming from that box ain't it? So now what do we do?" Jerry replied.

They approached the Ark but were stopped by a barrier. It was like a sheet of Perspex and there upon it were several hieroglyphic symbols. Jonny placed his hand on the Perspex. A loud hum could be heard.

"I can understand this, Jerry. It says, 'Welcome bold travellers, take great care... before you enter... and caution before you deactivate this shield'." At the end of this was the hieroglyphic symbol with a pulsating light.

"I think we have to touch this and we can then get to the power pack." Johnny said.

The device Johnny was carrying, now started to come into operation. And the device Jerry was carrying send a beam of light to the hieroglyphic symbol, the sheet of Perspex dissolved and they could now pass. Walking towards the Ark, the heavenly sounds got louder as if it was a jet engine powering up. Johnny's device started to glow and the sound died down, along with the brightness radiating from the Ark.

As they approached, the Ark slowly raised itself off the ground and could be seen hovering by itself.

"Can we touch it?" Jerry asked.

"I don't see why not. We are the ones who have been chosen to find it." Johnny said, touching the Ark.

As his hand was placed upon it, it slowly started to move.

"Look, Jerry. I think we can just push it to the ship."

"That's if it's still there. Oh, I do hope Mr Wrigley ain't pressed any buttons," he replied.

They started to manoeuvre the Ark back towards the craft, but it seemed to know its way already. It just floated by itself; all they had to do was guide it along and press the symbols on the walls as they approached them.

To their delight, the ship was still there and the outer door opened.

"Thank heavens you're back. There have been some very weird things happening in here." Mr Wrigley said as he was reaching up to remove his helmet.

"No! Don't take that off!" Johnny shouted.

"Now what?" he replied.

Just then, a box-like chamber came up from the floor. As it came to a stop, the front of it opened. "Place the power unit into here," the ship's voice said.

They quickly pushed the device into the box. Once it was inside, a light green glow came around the box and concealed it, then lowered back down into the floor.

After a few minutes the chamber once again filled with the purple mist and then slowly dissipated. "Your atmosphere is back to normal, it is safe to remove suits," said the ship's voice.

Johnny gingerly removed his helmet and took a deep breath.

"OK, it's safe to remove your helmets," he told them.

"I don't know, all this messing about just for that?" Mr Wrigley said.

"You haven't seen what we've seen," Jerry replied.

"Right, it's time we got out of here," replied Johnny.

"What is your destination?" asked the ship's voice.

"My farm. I've got the chickens to feed, they don't feed themselves." Mr Wrigley said.

The craft rose and the ship just dissolved through the pyramid wall and, in a flash, they were on the outside.

"Blimey, its daylight. And look at all the people."

"Yes but they aren't looking up at us. How strange is that?"

With the additional power, the ship had now got an invisibility shield and it could no longer be seen. The ship rose high up in the sky and turned in a northerly direction and made its way back to the farm. It kept to a low speed of around four thousand miles per hour so not to cause any shock waves.

Looking at the monitors, they could see the Mediterranean quickly disappearing behind them the coast of Spain and France was soon in sight.

"Look, Mr Wrigley, we are going over the channel."

"Tell me when we get back home, so I can open my eyes," he replied.

Jerry looked at Mr Wrigley; he had a hand over his eyes, but had a gap in between his fingers. "Don't be a baby, have a proper look."

Mr Wrigley lowered his hand. "Crikey, it's like being outside and it's a better picture than my telly," he replied.

The ship now reduced its speed as it started to enter British air space.

"Look at that, Jerry. Is that Heathrow?" asked Johnny.

"Could be. There's a lot of planes down there. Hey! You don't think they will come after us again do you?" Jerry asked.

"I don't think so, now the ship has full power it will be able to stop anything detecting it." Johnny replied.

"Wow! This is wonderful, lads. I wish I had watched it all the way," Mr Wrigley said.

The craft soon reached Mr Wrigley's farm and slowed down. It came to a hover over the mound of soil where had first crashed, five thousand years ago.

"Come on, lads, lets go and get a cuppa. You can put the kettle on and I'll put the chickens away." Mr Wrigley said.

The boys entered the farmhouse and put the kettle on. Jerry looked in the fridge and got out the milk. "Oh, I wonder if we should get the bread and cheese out and make a sandwich?" asked Jerry.

"That's a good idea, pass me the bread and cheese, oh and the butter. I'll make the sandwiches while you make a pot of tea." Johnny replied.

A short time after, Mr Wrigley returned carrying a basket of eggs.

"We have made some cheese sandwiches and a pot of tea."

"That's very good boys. I'm ready for a snack and a cuppa," he said, pulling out a chair next to the table.

"Can we tell you something, Mr Wrigley? You have been like a father to us."

"Well that's nice of you," he replied.

"Would you be mad if we said we are going with the ship?"

"What? Where to?" he screeched.

"Don't know! Wherever it takes us." Johnny replied.

"But I won't see you again, and you have," he stopped, took out his handkerchief and blow his nose. "You are like sons to me, I have never had such good friends for years, before you came I was about to end it all," he said, with tears trickling down his face.

"We will be back, in a week or two." Johnny said, holding back his tears.

"Yeah, it's only like going to the seaside." Jerry replied.

"Well, I'll keep the door open for you both, for when you get back." Mr Wrigley said, almost choking on his words. "When are you planning on leaving?"

"After we've had our sandwiches and a cuppa with you, Mr Wrigley."

"Well you have to do what you think is right, but you will be missed."

"You could come with us." Johnny said.

"No, who would look after the farm and the animals? No, I'll stay here and wait for you to return. You have been through all this so I think you have the right to visit where ever they came from." Mr Wrigley said.

Jerry jumped up. "Can I used your phone Mr Wrigley? I want to tell me mam."

"You can forget that, Jerry, there is no way am I going anywhere with your mam! God, she sends me mad." Johnny said.

"I just want to tell her we are going away for a while, just so she knows where we are," he replied.

"We? Ya mam can't stand me, she's always telling me off when I call for you."

"You know what I mean." Jerry replied, looking up at the ceiling.

So, after phoning home, the two lads said goodbye to their old friend and reassured him they would always remember their adventure together and he would always be in their thoughts.

They all walked out to the ship together, Mr Wrigley in the centre and the boys each side of him. As they walked towards the ship, Mr Wrigley took hold of their hands. As they reached the ship's entrance, Mr Wrigley turned to them both.

"I wish you would change your minds, but as I said I will

always be here for you."

The three friends hugged each other and were all teary eyed.

"We will really miss you, Mr Wrigley." Johnny said.

"Same here," replied Mr Wrigley.

They turned and entered the ship.

"Goodbye, Father." Jerry said as he turned to Mr Wrigley with tears rolling down his cheek while waving goodbye.

A few minutes later, the ship made a humming noise and slowly rose from its hover. The two lads waved to Mr Wrigley, although he couldn't see them. And at the same time, Mr Wrigley was waving back to them.

The ship climbed higher into the clear night sky. Mr Wrigley watched it until it was a faint dot in the clear sky and, with a blink of the eye, it had gone from sight.

The boys were wondering if they had made the right choice but as they looked back, the Earth was soon the size of a golf ball and then it had gone. They were now travelling in hyperspace and travelling towards their new home.

"So, as you can see, I'm not sure if this is what really happened, but one thing is for sure. Mr Wrigley passed away a year or two ago and, according to the local paper, in his will he left the farm, all the land and his money to his closest friends, Johnny Smith and Jerry Henshaw, which also said 'on their return'." Mr Johnson told the boys.

"Gosh, Dad, do you think it was true?" Tom asked excitedly.

"Well let's say the things they told me and what I saw, it certainly could have been. I remember them both going off at the weekends metal detecting together and they definitely had big lumps on their heads. And it was said in the local *Gazette* 'that a local boy had a power to heal the sick'."

"So do you think they went to space, Dad? and will they come back?" Jack asked.

"I don't know the answer to that one Jack, but all I do know is I haven't seen or heard from them since." Mr Johnson said, looking out the window up at the full Moon.

The End.
(Or is it?)